Ghost

Black Hawk MC
Book Four

by Carson Mackenzie

Published by CM Books, LLC
Copyright © April 2018 Carson Mackenzie
Cover Design by Carson Mackenzie
ISBN# 978-1-952184-32-1
ISBN# 978-1-078746-71-7
ISBN# 978-1-710345-37-7

Synopsis

Braxton "Ghost" Carver lost a lot in his life and struggled to find his way. If not for his friend and SEAL team member, Max Browning's suggestion of coming to Black Hawk MC with him, Brax wasn't sure whether he would have survived life's latest blow. However, even with acceptance from the club and the time he needed to heal, he wondered if his life would ever come into balance again.

Luna Wildflower Madison has been on her own for more years than she cared to count. Even when the Ops Warriors took her into their fold, she still felt as if something was missing and hadn't quite found her place in the world. Well, at least not until she runs into a friend from her past, one she never expected to see again.

Will a chance encounter bring two people a second chance? Or will life once again show how unkind it can be?

Table of Contents

Prologue

Ghost

The C-130 hit turbulence, and I immediately jerked awake. As I looked around the transport, I wasn't the only one the motion disturbed from sleep. The transport had been full when we left overseas, but the one we were on now was at half capacity for the second leg of our trip. My SEAL team had been lucky when we reached Germany and was able to hitch a ride to the States on the plane headed for Bragg. Once there, we disembarked and had enough time to stretch our legs before boarding again and taking off to the west coast. I couldn't have done better if I'd booked connecting flights with civilian carriers.

Our mission completed, with the added bonus of no injuries or casualties, made the hours spent in the air tolerable. Not like it mattered how long it took to get back to our home base, considering we'd already been awake for seventy-two hours. The bay door hadn't been secured before the other team members and I were out cold. The brief stopover at Bragg to change planes had been only a small disruption in our sleep. Now we were almost home.

"Damn, my neck is stiff as shit," my friend and team member, and the one in charge of our mission, Lieutenant Commander Max Browning, also nicknamed Flirt within the team, complained beside me as he rubbed his neck and yawned.

"Hell, be glad you have a neck."

"No joke. I'm surprised we pulled the shit off. That had the potential to be one huge fubar." Max had leaned in close and lowered his voice when he spoke, so there was no chance anyone not from our team would overhear. Especially since we sat along one side and faced the seats that ran down the middle of the plane's cargo area.

"As glad as I'll be to get back and see the family, I'm not looking forward to the Captain's debriefing." Flirt groaned at my mention of the Captain. Captain Baker was a perfectionist and expected nothing less from his men. He'd praise the job being done, but the man never failed to find the one thing that could have been done, foreseen, or executed better.

"Yeah, he isn't going to care about the flaw in the intel nor the end result of us completing this mission, even with the worthless information," Flirt mumbled disgustedly, and I chuckled.

"Nope, but you better believe he'll question the camels." I grinned, and Flirt flipped me off.

"Hey, we only borrowed them. It wasn't as if they had turned into casualties. The original plan went south, and we needed transportation, and they were there. I'd make the same call again if I had to."

"I'm not disagreeing, Max, but if the other teams hear about that shit, we will never live it down."

"Not me, because this is the last time I'll have to sit through this crap. As for shit from the other teams, they can kiss our asses. We have the best extraction record to date. It's not how the job is done, it's that the job gets done," Flirt said.

"True. Still can't believe you are calling it quits and processing out. Going to miss you, man," I said and bumped Flirt with my shoulder.

Max and I had hit it off from the get-go. We had a bond that superseded the one men on SEAL teams naturally shared with each other.

"Hey, not too late, bro. Don't re-up. Grab the ol' lady and kid and come with me, Brax."

"Maybe I'll head your way once I reach retirement if it's an open-end offer."

"Damn straight it's open. You've met a couple of my club brothers when they've visited. You'd fit right in at Black Hawk, Brax. But I'm hoping to see you before you retire. Nothing stopping you and the family from visiting."

"No, there's not. I'll visit just to make sure you're riding the straight and narrow."

"I'll be riding. That's for damn sure. Straight and narrow might be a stretch." Max and I chuckled just as the plane started its descent.

"Not long now," I said as I glanced down at my watch. "I want a hot shower and a meal that doesn't come out of a package or a machine."

"I'm hoping the Captain holds off until at least tomorrow before we have to talk with him. And where does the ol' lady and kid fall into your plans, Brax?" Max asked and lifted his brows.

"We aren't that lucky with the Captain. And other than a hug and kiss for both Stormy and BJ, there'll be no laying with the wife until I knock off a few layers of the grime and funk we got going on."

"Speak for yourself, fucker. I smell manly," Max said, and I rolled my eyes.

"Only to yourself," I yelled out over the sound of the C-130 as it touched down and hit the brakes to get the big bird to slow. It hadn't taken long before we were taxiing the runway.

The plane stopped, and as the engines started shutting down, the bay door was opening. I unfastened my harness and collected my backpack. When every team member was ready, we began filing out the back.

"I hope someone's already here to pick us up and we don't have to wait for them," Max said just as we reached the ramp.

"I checked in with the unit when we were killing time at Bragg. They said someone would be sent out. I'm hoping Stormy got the text I left her and shows up at the unit."

"Where's your truck?"

"She has it. Her car died, and I didn't have a chance to look at it before we left on the mission. As many times as the thing has broken down, I should junk it instead of putting more money into it. The warranty ran out, and the damn thing spends more time in the shop than it does in my driveway. Not to mention that operating with only one vehicle sucks ass," I said as we stepped off the ramp.

"Said you'd regret selling your bike."

"Yeah, said the single guy with no wife harping about between my job and the bike, she was destined to be a widow raising a young boy on her own."

Max laughed as we looked around at several different military vehicles to see if one was there for us.

"Wonder why the Captain's here?" I glanced at Max when he spoke, then followed his line of sight. Sure enough, the Captain's driver sat in the otherwise empty jeep that was parked alongside one of the unit's trucks that I assumed was there to pick us up.

"Just the driver. Don't see the Captain, though," I said and hoisted the strap of my bag higher on my shoulder.

"Hope to hell, Seaman Marks isn't here to inform us we have to go up to battalion now. Jinxed my ass with hoping Captain Baker would let us have a day or two," Max griped.

"You and the damn camels." I chuckled and slapped him on the shoulder.

"Fuck off," Max grumbled.

"I'd planned to after I had a nice, hot shower. Now that's going to be delayed." The others groaned in agreement with me as we moved toward the vehicles.

"LC, LT, I'm supposed to pick both of you up and take you to HQ. Captain Baker and Senior Chief Ross are waiting to speak with you," Seaman Marks said as he stepped out of the jeep when we approached. Max glanced at me, and I shrugged.

"They don't want everyone present?" Max asked.

"No, sir. I was told only you and Lieutenant Carver," Marks answered as he took our packs and tossed them in the back of the jeep, then slid back into the driver's seat.

"If you see my wife in the parking lot, tell her I'll be along shortly," I yelled to the others.

"No prob," was the reply from several of the team as they continued to the truck.

"What's the odds they just want to tell us job well done in private," Max said as I jumped in the back of the jeep while he slid into the passenger side.

"Yeah, that's a possibility." Max flipped me off without even turning around.

The ride to the building where the Captain's office was located hadn't taken long. Once Marks pulled into the spot in front and parked, Max and I were out of the vehicle and on our way inside. When we reached the office, the door was closed, and Max knocked.

"Enter!" was yelled and Max opened the door.

When we stepped through the open door, the Captain and Senior Chief stood from their chairs. After formalities were over, the Captain waved to the chairs in front of his desk and Max and I sat as did he and Senior Chief.

"Carver, the Senior Chief and I needed to speak with you, and we thought it best if Browning was present. We know the two of you are close outside of the team."

I frowned and nodded in agreement with the Captain.

The Captain and Senior Chief looked at each other, then the Captain turned back and spoke directly to me, "Approximately two hours ago, we were notified by the local authorities about an accident involving your vehicle—"

"Where are they?" I asked, cutting the Captain off as I jumped to my feet. "Were they hurt? Are they at the hospital?" I raised my hand and ran it over my chest as a jab of pain hit.

Max stood and placed a hand on my shoulder. The Captain and Senior Chief were out of their chairs and on their feet, too. I needed to hear them say it, even though their facial expressions spoke volumes.

"Tell me," I whispered in a voice that sounded nothing like mine.

"I'm sorry, Carver," Senior Chief said and clasped my shoulder with his hand. "Your wife and son didn't make it. They died on impact."

I dropped down into the chair and closed my eyes. Stormy's and BJ's faces were automatically there as I listened to Captain Baker and Senior Chief tell everything they knew about the accident.

Max's hand was strong as he squeezed my shoulder and lent me his strength and support. At that moment, though, I wasn't sure it was enough to get me through the loss.

I wasn't sure anything could.

Chapter One

Ghost

"No, don't go!" The scream had my eyes snapping open. I laid there and caught my breath before I sat up on the side of the bed and wiped my hands down my face. Damn dream. The squeal of tires. The grinding sound of metal. It was as if I'd been there when the crash happened. When in all actuality it was how I'd pictured the accident that had taken Stormy and BJ after I saw the condition of the truck and read the accident report from the police. Two innocent lives lost when the guy with the blood alcohol level double the legal limit got on the freeway headed in the wrong direction. He walked away with a few bruises from his seatbelt and the airbag as it disengaged.

The dream this time had been different, though. Where before it ended with me viewing their bodies and saying goodbye, it changed to the three of us standing on the beach, facing the sun. Stormy and BJ started to walk away hand-in-hand as if headed toward the sun. A good bit away, they stopped and turned their heads, looked at me and smiled. BJ gave a small wave and Stormy blew a kiss. When they turned back, they continued to walk away until the rays from the sun absorbed them.

"Shit, why now?" I stood and walked into the bathroom. After I relieved myself and splashed cold water on my face, I went back into the bedroom, then into the closet and pulled on a pair of sweatpants and a sweatshirt. Never once did I allow my eyes to drift to the shelf above my head that held the two intricately carved boxes. My daily reminder of everything I lost. Instead, I donned my running shoes and walked out of the room. Off the small table by the door, I grabbed my cell and keys, then stepped out into the dark.

Once the door was locked, I shoved both in the pocket of my sweatshirt, pulled the hood up and over my head, and took off at a run. Nothing like breathing crisp air into your lungs to clear your head.

Dawn was still a couple hours away, but I made my way down the sidewalk and through the neighborhoods by the glow of the streetlights. Only a couple of houses I passed had lights on inside. Other than that, it was just me, my thoughts, and plenty of pavement to pound my feet on.

Wasn't sure how long I ran, but I continued to push my body. It was familiar, the burn in my chest, the ache of my muscles. I'd ran like this every day for the first six months after I arrived. It centered me. Between my activities with the club and the simple acceptance from the men, I slowly healed. To find my way back.

So, why now? Deep in the surface of my mind, I knew what had brought the change in the dream. The trip I made with Devil and Jag to return Jas back to the Ops.

That day had been just another long ass day on the road until we finally pulled into San Jose. Found the motel where we would stay overnight and snagged our rooms. It was my first long haul as a patched member with Black Hawk, and I couldn't even complain about making the trip inside a cage instead of on my bike. Because I owed the club a lot for taking in the broken man I was when I arrived with Flirt those months back.

We hadn't been at the motel long when we heard the rumble of pipes in the distance. Two came into view while an SUV had followed behind them. When Jas had jumped up and down, I figured it had to be her people. They pulled in and the two men on the bikes dismounted, and when the one got both his feet on the ground, he had just enough time to catch Jas as she jumped into his arms. Jas finished with one and moved to the next man and did the same as two women stepped out of the SUV.

That was the moment everything around me centered on the short-haired blonde. I heard everyone's voices and the things they had said, but I hadn't given a shit about any of it. My only interest had been on the woman.

"Luna?" I asked, and the woman turned her head away from Jas and looked at me.

"Oh. My. God. Braxton Samuel Carver!" she yelled and more talking from the others followed. There'd been questions from the other woman about me. I knew my own brothers were curious, but I hadn't taken my eyes off Luna for fear she'd disappear.

The other woman called her Moon instead of Luna and was going on about shit. She'd even stepped in front of Luna as if to protect her from me. As if that was ever a worry.

I'd narrowed my eyes at the woman as she ranted about getting her knives and when her focus moved to one of the men when he spoke to her, I grabbed Luna's arm and headed toward my motel room.

I closed the motel's door behind us, and it had been the first feeling I had that maybe life hadn't forgotten about me.

Now, as I headed down the sidewalk to my place, it was hard for me to believe that it had been almost a month since I saw Luna. Touched her. Ran my hands over her body. The phone calls weren't enough, and the distance between us was too far. I needed to work on a plan to change that. I needed Luna like the air I was taking into my lungs. Second chances were rare, and no way was I going to let mine pass me by.

By the time I was back inside my place, my body was no longer strained and exhausted. It was exhilarated. With my mind clear, I stripped the sweaty clothes from my body and stepped into the shower.

Thirty minutes later, I was unlocking the back door to the pawnshop. Been too long since I looked forward to doing a job, instead of just something to keep my mind occupied so I could forget.

Life was for living, wasn't it? And somewhere between my last days in the military and now, I seemed to have forgotten that.

Chapter Two

Luna

I thought I'd put one of the worst days of my life behind me for the most part. But I'd been wrong, and I knew it the moment he said my name. Braxton Carver. He'd been a friend, a neighbor, and the first and only man to stomp on my heart. The funny part, he hadn't even known he'd done it. When I looked up at the six foot five man in front of me that day, I cataloged every visible change in him from the last time I'd seen him. He sported a shaved head, instead of the close-cut military style that had at least shown some of his black hair. But the biggest change in him had been his gray eyes. Where they once shined with warmth, humor, and kindness, they were harder, and the hurt in their depths almost had made me stagger back.

Today wasn't the first time I wondered if I would have made the trip with the others to San Jose to pick up Jas if I'd known Brax was going to be one of the men from Black Hawk at the meet. Then again, I hadn't known he'd become a part of them in the first place.

When I recognized him, the voices around turned to muffled sounds. I knew Harmony was talking and that she probably wanted to know who and where I knew Brax from, but I couldn't bring myself to answer her. Hell, I hadn't even protested when Brax grabbed my arm and led me away from the others.

Probably because I knew Harmony would figure it out. The Lady Riders knew my story. Thanks to one drunken girls' night and a bottle of tequila. Lesson learned, and I hadn't touched tequila since.

My initial shock of running into him that day had ended with the click of a motel room door and the sound of a lock being thrown.

"What the hell are you doing, Brax?" I asked with as much attitude as I could muster.

"What am I doing? What the hell are you doing with the Ops, Luna? Is that where you've been this whole time? Christ, even Stormy hadn't known where you went. Fuck, we were friends, and you couldn't be bothered to keep in touch?" Brax demanded, ran his hand over his head, then across the back of his neck. He acted like I owed him an explanation of how I lived my life.

Then, I didn't have to find my attitude. It was there.

"How are your wife and kid?" I asked with a bite to my tone that even I heard. And at the time, I hadn't given two shits if the statement was fair or not. Or that Brax had no clue what had happened.

"Dead." His single word had me taking a seat on the bed.

"How? When?" I asked, my voice softer than just seconds ago.

"Head-on collision the day I landed from a mission. Stormy and BJ were on their way to welcome me home. A drunk changed that. It's going on a year since it happened." Brax sat down beside me on the bed and leaned his elbows on his knees and dropped his head.

"I'm sorry, Brax," I said, and he nodded, but kept his head bent.

"Thanks." It was quiet for a minute until Brax spoke again, "She told me, you know? Everything."

"What?" I whispered.

"Why didn't you say anything that last day, instead of letting me leave for BUD/S (Basic Underwater Demolition/SEAL) school, thinking everything was fine?" After he asked, he turned his face toward me, and the pain in his eyes took my breath.

"Does it really matter, Brax? Any of it?" I stood. I needed to put distance between us. "It was years ago. I had no claim on you, just feelings that I didn't act on. Then it was too late. What was I supposed to do on your last day home on leave? Tell you, 'Hey, Brax, saw you and Stormy fucking and oh, by the way, I've had a crush on you for the past two years and catching the two of you broke my heart.' Would that have helped in the long run? Would it have stopped you from marrying Stormy when you found out she was pregnant?" I stopped pacing and looked at Brax and ran my hand over my short, blond hair. From the

look of sadness on his face, I knew I wasn't going to like his answer, but he wouldn't have been the Brax I remembered if he had given me the answer I wanted.

"No, it wouldn't have stopped me. Even if you had told me your feelings, the results would have still been the same when I found out Stormy was carrying my kid. And yeah, I know you can be an active parent without marriage, but I was raised to take responsibility for my actions. You knew my parents. They were great together. My dad had married my mom after he had done twenty years in the service. I was the later in life baby surprise that happens." Brax stood and walked until he was in front of me.

"Stormy told me after we married that you two had a fight over something stupid and she'd known you had feelings for me, so when she ran into me while I was out with some of the guys, she volunteered to drive me home. I told her I was meeting you in the parking lot at the cinema complex. That you and I were going to see a movie for my last night in town and she said she would drive me there and wait with me until you got there. I can give you a hundred lame excuses for fucking her in her car, but like you said, doesn't really make a difference now, does it?"

"No, so I don't understand why you pulled me into this room. It's all in the past."

"Is that why you took off after you graduated high school?"

I knew I could lie, but what was the use? While each of my friends was finding their men, I often wondered if it was the past that kept me from settling down, instead of jumping beds with the men from the Ops. Not like I did that as often as some of the other single women.

"When Stormy admitted she was pregnant, I knew I couldn't be there when you came back to marry her." Brax frowned down at me, *and I continued, "We grew up together, Brax. We were friends. I knew you would do right by her and the baby. But I couldn't be there to watch it. I graduated and took off. Traveled around for about six months, waitressing when I needed to earn some more money before moving on until I ended up in Riverton, Nevada. I took a waitress job in town at a small diner, and it was a place the Ops frequented. I was there about a month, got to know some of the Ops women and they told me I could make a shit ton of money stripping and dancing at Bitches, the Ops' club, so I did. Before I knew it, I was part of the Ops and have been ever since." I shrugged.*

"Is that what you're doing now? Stripping for a bunch of bikers?"

It was my turn to frown at Brax's tone. I wouldn't apologize for anything I chose in my life, not to Brax or anyone else.

"When I want to, but that isn't any of your business. Like I said before, I didn't have a claim on you, and you don't have one on me. I'm a Lady Rider. I can damn fucking well do exactly what I want. If I want to strip, I strip. If I want to fuck one of the men, I fuck him. I imagine it's no different with you since you're part of Black Hawk. I know they have a strip club and you're a single male. Bet your bed doesn't stay cold long." I was being bitchy, and I didn't give a damn. Being shut in that room with Brax brought feelings back I had long ago put to rest.

"Goddammit, Luna—"

"It is Moon now, Ghost. Isn't that what they called you?" I interrupted him, and he sneered.

"What. The. Fuck. Ever." He stepped forward, and I took a step back and hated myself for it. I wasn't scared of the big man; I never had been.

"Don't cop an attitude with me. I don't have to stand here and put up with shit," I snapped, turned toward the door, and that was as far as I got before huge hands grabbed my arms. There was no time for me to protest before I was spun around and facing Brax while he held me at arm's length and looked down at me.

"No, you don't, but you're going to listen, anyway. We've been friends since I was seven and you were five, living next door to each other. I got used to looking after you, thought of you as a little sister." I went to jerk out of his hands, because that was just what every woman wanted to hear from a man, but Brax was having none of it. He pulled me into him until I had to bend my head back to look up at him. "Let me finish. Fuck, I don't remember you being so damn prickly when we were growing up."

"Fuck you, Brax. Let me go." I refused to listen to anything more that proved my feelings for him were stupid and those of a naïve young girl. I was far from that girl.

"Yeah, like I haven't thought of that a few hundred times over the years. I can tell by your expression that shocks the hell out of you and has left you speechless. Let's see if I can stun you a little more. Like I was saying, I thought of you as a little sister until you hit puberty, then that went out the window right fucking quick. I will thank you for the patience you taught me because every time I was around you, all I wanted to do was strip you down. Lun... Moon, it was like I went to bed one night and you were my pal, then the next day you had curves and breasts, which to a sixteen-year-old boy is everything good in the world."

I hadn't thought I could laugh, but I did because Brax had closed his eyes and his face had looked pained. When he opened his eyes back up, they were filled with want and desire for me. My stomach tightened then and now with just the thought of him. I'd wondered briefly how the hell I had ever put the man out of my head for a minute over the years. He'd meant everything to me back then. Maybe too much.

"I wouldn't risk our friendship because, Moon, I don't think I could have lived with myself, but if I would have known that staying away from you was going to cost me years without yo—"

"Brax," I whispered when he stopped before finishing the sentence.

"Sorry, I can't say that because if I had gone after you, I wouldn't have had BJ, my son. I would never wish him away, not even for time with you, Moon. Stormy and I had a rocky start, but I grew to love her, she was the mother of my child. I mourned the loss of them, but the hardest part for me was wondering if I didn't love her enough and that's why she and BJ were taken away from me. It took me a while to realize that was just stupidity on my part, and my brothers," Brax pointed to the door in the direction of the men outside, *"they helped more than I can ever repay. There is nothing I can say to change the fact Stormy and I... well, I'd been drinking with the guys and feeling a little sorry for myself because I was heading back out the next morning. Wishing you had graduated already so I could talk you into going back with me. I fucked up bad. I didn't want Stormy then, I wanted you. After I left, I'd plan to finish BUD/S school and my basic parachute jumping course and come back for you and tell you my feelings. That plan died when Stormy called me a month later and said she was pregnant. You were gone when I came back to marry her."* Brax stopped to take a deep breath, and I laid my head on his chest.

"I've lost enough, team members, my parents, my son. I'm sorry too that you lost your mom. But when you stepped in front of me in the parking lot, the first thing I thought was there is my best friend, then I remembered you took off and why. It still didn't keep me from getting pissed off." Brax let go of me, and I took a step back, then looked up at him.

"What is wrong with the women at Black Hawk?" I asked.

"Nothing. What the fuck does that have to do with anything?" Brax asked and frowned.

"I think there is. Blind and stupid come to mind if not one of those women figured out a fucking teddy bear is in that big ass body of yours." I didn't give Brax a chance to reply, I raised my arms and grabbed his face with my hands and brought it down to mine. When our lips touched, I felt the change in Brax. I didn't hold my control long, either. After he devoured my mouth, he pulled back slightly.

"No, they just weren't you," Brax said and captured my mouth again. I opened, and he took. I gave, and he took more.

Brax's big hands pulled my top up, and he only broke the kiss to pull it over my head. He tossed it. My bra was next, then my breasts spilled into his hands, and he groaned into my mouth, and I whimpered into his.

Lost, I thought, in him.

We moved in a frenzy as clothes were removed and then, naked, we fell on the bed with me on top. Brax touched me everywhere, and it still wasn't enough. I could feel his hardened length pressed against my center, and I needed the connection. Wanted it more than my next breath.

I pushed off Brax's chest and rose to my knees and straddled him. As I watched his gray eyes darken, I wrapped my hand around his *cock and moved it to my entrance. When I had his cock lined up, I sank down and took him inside me. I felt the burn as his size stretched me to the point of pain, but after I let myself adjust, I began to move, and the pain was replaced with pure pleasure.*

"Goddamn, I'm not going to last. You're so wet and tight, and you feel so fucking good," Brax gritted out between his teeth, and I picked up the pace.

My back arched as Ghost squeezed and tweaked my nipples. When he moved one hand down, thrust his hips up to meet my downward motion, and pinched my clit, I exploded. I threw my head back, and the scream that echoed in the room was followed by a groan. I felt his cock swell, then the warmth of his release filled me.

I collapsed on Ghost's chest, and he wrapped his arms around me. Right as I snuggled into him and was ready to drop off to sleep, it hit me, and my eyes flew open.

"Oh my God, we didn't use a condom!"

"Yeah, worst day ever my ass!" I said and leaned over the toilet for round two. My stomach was tightening for a whole different reason this time, and I wasn't quite sure how I felt about it.

Chapter Three

Ghost

"Damn, you started early."

I tightened the last anchor to the wall before I turned and looked at Roscoe as he walked in the back door of the pawnshop.

I glanced at my watch. "It's almost ten."

"Yeah, and by the looks, you're almost done, which means you were in here at the butt crack of dawn. You need a woman, then your ass wouldn't be so eager to get out of bed in the mornings."

"Some of us aren't lucky enough to snag a woman like Sue."

"Damn straight. I'm a lucky bastard and am not ashamed to admit it, either."

"Probably good, since Sue doesn't strike me as the type to let you forget it, Roscoe."

Roscoe chuckled, "Nah, she definitely isn't. The woman has never been one to hold back on words or a good cast iron skillet if the need calls." Roscoe then moved to grab the board I had leaned against the wall. I bent and lifted the bottom, and with his help, we placed it on the anchors and slid it into place.

"Keeps you in line with the skillet, does she?" I chuckled as we placed another board.

"Ah, no need for her to threaten me. I'm an agreeable sort. Especially when it comes to getting laid regularly."

"I could've gone the rest of my life without that knowledge," I groaned, and Roscoe laughed.

"That's what's wrong with young people. Ya think you've got the corner on warming the sheets."

Christ, at that point, I had no desire to get into a discussion on geriatric sex. I picked up the electric screwdriver and the screws and began fastening the shelves to the anchors, but even the noise wasn't enough to keep Roscoe quiet.

"When ya find the one woman who will put up with your sorry ass and accept everything about you, you hold on. That's why I'm moving in with Sue. After I lost my wife, I'd accepted I wouldn't find another woman that would even come close. Known Sue for a long time. Wolf was a good man and husband to her, and I don't think she was looking for a replacement either, but fate is a funny thing. Second chances don't come around as often as folks think. Sure, you might find someone you're comfortable with, but to find everything in another person who fits you is not too common. Just because the love might be different, doesn't mean it's wrong. Anyway, the cabin's almost empty now. Only got a few things left there. You should ask Prez if you can move in."

"What would I need all that space for? It's just me." I placed another screw on the shelf and out of the corner of my eye, Rosco shook his head.

"Young folks," I heard him mumble before he turned and walked out of the storeroom into the main part of the shop.

"Jesus, for a bunch of bikers, everyone sure is gossipy," I said out loud to the empty room, finished the last shelf, and placed the tools back in the box. When my phone vibrated, I pulled it out of my pocket and slid my thumb across the screen before I lifted it to my ear.

"Yo."

"Your phone skills are exemplary, brother," Flirt said, then chuckled.

"Caller ID, dickhead. Not like I didn't know it was you. What's up?" I asked.

"Now is that how to talk to an officer of the club? You always have had a problem with authority figures."

"Oh, that is rich, brother. Besides, after you slept with someone a few hundred times, shouldn't you be more relaxed with them?"

When no response came from Flirt, I laughed.

"Holy shit, Brax, did you crack a joke?"

"What can I say? I'm one fucking happy guy."

"Oh, yeah, we should have called you Happy." Flirt's sarcastic comment made me laugh harder.

"Did you call to harass my ass, or is there a point to this phone call?"

"Where you at now? Home?"

"Nah, I had some time this morning, so I'm at Buy and Sell. I put the extra shelving up in the back that Roscoe needed."

"If you've finished, come to the clubhouse, we want to talk with you."

"You got it. Won't be long, only need to sweep up," I said and grabbed the broom out of the small utility closet.

"See you a few, brother," Flirt said, and the phone clicked, signaling he had disconnected.

It hadn't taken long for me to clean the storage area. And after I let Roscoe know I was leaving, I went out the back door and got on my bike and headed to the clubhouse.

As I rode up to the gate at Black Hawk, the newest prospect stepped out of the guard hut. Lock pledged in right after Devil, Jag, and I had gotten back from San Jose. Now that had been a fucking trip. I hadn't been the only one who had a life-changing experience that week. Devil came back to the compound with a sister he hadn't even known existed.

I slowed the bike enough to give Lock the time to roll the gate open. After a chin lift, I hit the throttle and rode through. The short stretch of road to the clubhouse hadn't taken long before I was parked and dismounted.

By the time I reached the building, squeals and laughter stopped me in my tracks. When I turned my head in the direction the sounds came from, Ally and Neely popped into sight from the side of the clubhouse. Ally was on her bike and Neely pedaling her little legs to keep up as she followed behind on a pink bicycle with training wheels. They spotted me and smiled.

"Hey, ladies. How's it going?" I asked as they stopped and got off their rides. I smiled when I got a good look at them.

Ally wore jeans, little biker boots, and a black t-shirt with a blue jean vest that had Spider Monkey stitched where the name tag would be. Neely wore tiny Keds, a fluffy skirt with a ton of colors, and a pink t-shirt with the same blue jean vest over it, but her stitching said Lil' Sis.

"Hey, Ghost," Ally yelled from the spot where they parked their bikes. I had to give them points. The bicycles sat in a spot between several other bikes. The ones that ran on gas instead of leg power and would have tipped if the girls hadn't taken care of parking theirs.

I squatted as they approached me. "Nice day for a ride."

"Yeah, 'cept I had to ride my bike because Neely can't have a motorcycle yet," Ally said, then looked over her shoulder at Neely.

"I's learning. Then I get a bike like yours. Dev said I would," Neely answered Ally, but looked at me when she said the last part.

Neely might have been shy in the beginning, but it sure hadn't lasted long. It seemed being with Devil and Bailey; she was coming out of her shell. Her speech was improving, too. She had a rough start to her life living with her mom. That was until Devil found her in that house dirty and in clothes too small, with his mother's pimp/drug dealer, or whatever the creep was to the woman. Neely's life definitely took a turn for the better that day. I never wanted to imagine what would have happened if Devil hadn't come across her.

Especially after the scum wanted to sell her to Devil, and Devil found out she was his sister. The asshole paid for that physically by fists, then later when he was picked up for having kiddy porn on his computer. I figured he probably wished he'd chosen better in his life since most prisons' population wasn't known to have much tolerance for those who messed with kids.

As for the mom, she'd signed her rights away to Devil since she was on her way to being incarcerated on drug charges and wouldn't be out anytime soon. Not that I figured Devil would ever let the woman around Neely again.

"If you hurry and learn, you can get rid of them baby wheels."

"They ain't baby wheels. Dev said it's so I don't get hurt when I's fall."

I fought the twitching of my lips, not wanting to laugh and chance hurting Neely's feelings.

"Dev said, huh?"

"Yep. Bailey said no, but me need a real bike to be a biker baby. That's what Dev said."

I wasn't able to hold in my laughter any longer.

"I think you mean *biker babe*."

Neely and Ally both looked at me and frowned, then Ally placed her hands on her hips.

"That's what she said."

I stood and shook my head. No way was I going to argue with two females. Even small ones.

"Your daddy and the others inside?" I asked Ally.

"Yep, Daddy sent us out because my papa was on the phone yelling at him."

"That so? Well, you two—"

"What's a... a unchic?" Ally cut me off and asked.

"A what?" I frowned at her.

"My papa said if Daddy don't marry my momma soon, he's gonna make him an unchic."

I chuckled when I realized what Ally was trying to pronounce. The two little girls looked up at me, expecting an answer that I was in no way going to give.

"Well, umm... it—" The door opened, and Flirt and Speed stepped outside, saving me.

"We heard you pull up and wondered what was taking you so long to come in. Now, I see. You're out here chatting up the babes," Flirt said, and Ally and Neely giggled.

I shook my head. Flirt had always had a way with women. Evidently, it was females of all ages.

"Nah, Ally was just asking me what a eunuch is," I said, and Flirt and I laughed when Speed groaned.

"Don't worry about that. And for God's sake, don't tell your mother that."

"Okay," Ally said and kicked at the ground.

"Now, are you two staying out of trouble?" Speed asked.

"Uh huh," Ally answered, then bit her lip.

"You sure about that?" Speed asked and lifted his brow. Ally nodded. I looked at Flirt and his lips were twitching as he looked between the two girls.

I did not know what they were going to be busted for, but to witness the interaction would be enjoyable. It always was.

"Neely?" Speed turned away from Ally and focused on Neely. Neely looked up at Speed and smiled but didn't say a word.

Speed looked between the two girls, then shook his head. Something was definitely up.

"Alright. Let's go about this differently. Have you two been inside the clubhouse? Maybe the kitchen?"

Watching the girls closely was the only reason I caught the slightest break in Ally's expression, and then it was masked just as quickly. Damn, Speed and Sami were in for some long, rough teenage years.

Father and daughter had a brief stare down until Ally smiled.

"Neely had to go potty. And we was hungry."

"So, you ate half a plate of cookies even though your momma told you they were for *after* lunch," Speed said, then sighed heavily.

"That's why we didn't eat them all," Ally said triumphantly, then she looked at Speed and sighed heavily. "Do you gotta tell Momma about the cookies?"

"I should because you didn't listen to what she told you," Speed said, and Ally pursed her lips and nodded.

"Okay, I'll listen better," Ally mumbled.

"Good, it will keep you out of trouble." Speed ran his hand down Ally's hair and pulled on her ponytail.

"Is that why papa wants to make you an unchic, because you didn't listen?" Ally asked.

"I don't think it has anything to do with not listening," Flirt said under his breath, and my lips twitched.

Speed closed his eyes, pinched his nose between two fingers, then rubbed his hand down his face.

"Ah hell, just stay close and out of trouble and I won't tell your mom about the cookies," Speed said with a sigh at the girls. Ally smiled, then both girls nodded and ran back to their bikes.

We watched them get on the bikes before we turned to go inside the clubhouse.

"Christ, I may not live to see that girl reach adulthood," Speed said, and Flirt and I laughed as we walked in.

"She'd make a helluva negotiator. She can take over as the club attorney when Jag wants to step down." Flirt laughed. "On a good note, fifty percent chance you get a boy this time," Flirt said and slapped Speed on the back.

"I'm sure that's comforting, brother. He had fifty percent the first time, too," I said and then laughed when Speed glared at Flirt.

"Fucker, I hope when you have kids that your ol' lady fills your house with girls. See how you and your dominant ass deals then," Speed said.

"They'll listen to me just like their mother will," Flirt said and tapped on the door to the prez's office, then opened it.

"Keep telling yourself that, brother. I hope you have a sense a humor because I'm going to sell tickets so everyone can watch your daughters run over your ass. And you will have daughters because I firmly believe in Karma," Speed said as we walked in and the others glanced at us.

We joined Crusher, Devil, Coast, and Jag at the table that sat off to one side.

"A sense of humor about what?" Crusher asked and leaned back in his chair.

Speed caught the others up and when he finished, they were laughing, too, and Flirt glared at us.

"If, and I mean *if*, I have girls, you brothers will see how it is done," Flirt said, sat back in his chair and crossed his arms over his chest, which only made us laugh harder.

"Oh, brother, gonna enjoy watching," Speed said and sat beside me, then turned to Devil. "And next time you can go deal with my daughter and Neely."

"Please, when Neely doesn't want to answer, she just smiles at you," Devil said, then chuckled. "Why do ya think I let you go out to handle it in the first place?"

"Okay, let's get this meeting started and just agree that no matter what age the females are we'll never have control," Crusher said, and we laughed, but not one of us disagreed.

Crusher's phone rang as he opened a folder in front of him. When he answered and started talking, the rest of us sat back and listened. Taking in the one-sided part of the conversation, it sounded as if the meeting was going to be delayed a little longer.

Chapter Four

Luna

The other Lady Riders and I listened as Creed informed us of security measures the club implemented to ensure there wouldn't be a hit on the compound. Since the Black Hearts were already in California, it was just a matter of time before they came knocking on our door. After the shit with Rebel, it was only going to piss them off more, which meant when they came here, it was going to get bloody. I wondered if we were ever going to have peace again.

As the men asked questions and continued to talk, the less I listened, and the more I focused on not tossing my lunch. The club had too much going on to add my little issue to the mix. Especially since I wasn't ready to share the information.

When I heard Sledge mentioned, I shook my head. It was still hard for some of us to believe that he used his old club to advance himself within the Black Hearts leadership until he held the president's spot. Because of that asshole, Fork's half-brother was shot in the mix and had to be transferred out of the town. Our men still hadn't found a trace of where the club went. It was as if the wind carried them off. The only good thing to come out of it all had been getting Raven back. Even after it all was said and done, we still had no clue what the hell set the Black Hearts on our tail in the first place. But whatever it was, it wasn't over.

"A few of their members have been spotted outside of San Diego," Creed said, then raised his hand to stop Harmony, who was prepared to speak. "I know what you're going to ask, and no, we didn't grab them. But it means they're getting closer."

"Why the hell did you not grab their worthless asses? We could be torturing the bastards right now, and that would send a message to the others that we aren't just going to sit around and wait to see what happens. Fuck that!" Harmony crossed her arms over her chest and sat back against the chair.

Rebel leaned forward and held out her hand to Harmony to give her a fist bump, then said, "Hell yeah, we could have. I don't mind adding that I dislike this whole, women remain in the background shit."

I was surprised the meeting hadn't gotten out of hand then. But I knew it would before it was over. No meeting with the women and men together ever ended peacefully.

I saw Shark's eyes roll before he pulled Rebel back in between him and Blade and then he snapped loudly, "Dammit, we are not discussing this anymore."

"It is going to be some long ass months with Harmony's hormones. You know that, brother?" Fork leaned over and mumbled to Creed, but it wasn't low enough, and Harmony glared at him while a few of the men tried not to laugh.

I'd been a part of the Ops Warrior MC for years. Nevertheless, it amazed me that the men had no clue about their women. Paybacks came in many different ways, and Fork and Creed would pay in spades by the time Harmony got done with them.

"Enough! Can we get through this meeting without all the bullshit and drama? And would you quit saying that, Fork, you know she wants to stab you in the eye every fucking time you repeat it. And she won't do it while you sleep, either," Creed said and pinched the bridge of his nose between his finger and thumb.

By the stress reflected in Creed's face, it surprised me he hadn't snapped before now. When the entire room went quiet at his tone, I knew he wasn't the only one on edge. The seriousness of the situation could be gauged by the dangerousness radiating off the men in the room. Like the ones who looked as though they stood casually leaning back against the wall, to someone who didn't know them, they could pass as men without a care in the world. An observant person would notice the men stood in strategic places around the room: off to each side of the windows, beside the two entrances into the room. Even the ones who sat in chairs were positioned to see through the doorways or out the windows. I also noticed that each man was positioned to where the other women and I were surrounded and covered if a threat occurred.

I saw that each man's eyes shone with knowledge, awareness, and danger that, if unleashed, would destroy anything in its path. My stomach rolled again at the thought, and I rubbed my hand across it, then tuned back in to listen to Creed.

"When the Black Hearts hit Ricco's place, they depleted the club's numbers, but not totally. Intel shows Sledge was able to build the club back using every piece of scum he could recruit. Black Hearts outnumber us even with the Furies added into the mix. If we leave half of our men back to protect the compounds, the Black Hearts will outnumber us two to one. We already know they had those men in LA who have disappeared, so more than likely they are here or close by. Considering the number of men, it would have to be a large place they're hiding in. Or they split up. Either way, we need to find them if we want the upper hand. Any questions or thoughts?" Creed asked and looked around the room.

"We could help secure the compound to free up some men, Creed," Shady commented, and all eyes cut to her. From the looks, I knew not one man would let the Lady

Riders fill in. "What? We can handle a gun or knives." Shady looked at Harmony and winked before she continued. "As well as some of you."

"That won't be happening, Shay," Cajun replied from his spot across the room, and I saw Shady stiffen, then her mouth open. Thank God Creed noticed too, because he raised his hand and stepped in before the meeting took another turn. At that point, I just wished they would finish because my stomach refused to settle down.

"Shay, no man in this room questions that you and your girls can't take care of business, but goddammit, we won't take that chance. Ever. Now several of you are carrying the next generation, so give us a fucking break and let us take care of you without giving us shit over it," Creed said and looked at each woman.

"Fine, as long as you know we won't be locked away while the crap's hitting the fan." Shady relaxed back in her seat.

"No one would expect anything less," Creed said, and the men in the room chuckled.

That had to have been a huge worry off the men's shoulders, because the air in the room actually felt lighter. I almost felt bad for my part in some of their distress over the years until Fork opened his mouth.

"We could even up the odds if Black Hawk would lend some support," Fork said and cocked his brow.

"They took great care of Jas, brother. A lot of their members have specialized training like us, too," Cajun brought up.

"Black Hearts wouldn't be expecting it," Kink added.

Other shit was said, but after they had mentioned Black Hawk, their voices sounded as if they were in a tunnel. Before I had time to think, I was up and on the move. When I reached the bathroom, I kicked the door shut and dropped to my knees with my head bent over the toilet. I realized the time I wanted to get used to my situation had run out.

The door opened, and the water turned on and off, and I was thankful for the cold cloth that was placed on the back of my neck. After I finished and rose, Harmony handed me another cloth to wipe my face. The coolness felt good on my skin and settled the last of my upset stomach.

"How long have you known?" Harmony asked.

"A couple of weeks when I missed my period, but I didn't want to believe it. I mean, come on, one time without a condom. Then the morning sickness started, and I couldn't deny it." My voice sounded almost defeated to myself.

"Sweetie, are you scared whoever it belongs to won't want it?" Boo asked and frowned.

"Tell us who, and we will make damn fucking sure they take responsibility. Not using a fucking condom, the asshole should know better. Who the fuck is it?" Shady ranted, and I knew she wouldn't hesitate to light one of the men up for being so careless.

"Shay, it, well..." I started, then stopped. I blew out a breath to relax, but I didn't get to finish before Harmony jumped in.

"Oh my God, it's the big guy's! That is why you ran out when the men mentioned Black Hawk. It is, isn't it?"

Harmony stared at me along with Boo and Shady. A seasoned spy would crack under their scrutiny.

Since I stood no chance of sidestepping them, I whispered, "Yes."

"Then what is the problem? I saw how he was with you when we left. Moon, that man loves you, and no one can convince me otherwise. Plus, I know he has been calling you since we've been back," Harmony crossed her arms over her chest and cocked her brow as if she waited for me to argue her point.

"Yeah, because we are friends. I told you he married my friend because she was pregnant—" I started, and Shady interrupted.

"Asshole is fucking married? Yeah, he needs to come here so I can kick his ass," Shady said and picked up the wet cloth on the counter and threw it. The splat sounded, and we each turned and watched the wet cloth slide to the floor.

"Wow, I thought my hormones were in overdrive," Harmony chuckled, and Shady glared at her.

"No, he's a widower. Brax lost his wife and son in a car accident. I've loved him since I was five. He was my best friend, and when... You know the story. I don't want him to think I expect marriage or anything from him. It was as much my fault as his for forgetting the condom." I looked at the women and they stared back at me for a minute without a word. Then Shady, Harmony, and Boo burst out laughing. I hadn't expected that response. "I don't think any of this is funny," I said, which only made the women laugh harder.

"Oh, Moon, do you really think you will have a choice when you tell him? Have you learned nothing about being a Lady Rider? We may make the men's lives a living hell, but in the end, they always get what they want." Shady was the first to compose herself enough to speak.

"Ops has been a big part of my life. I can't imagine him giving up his club, so to be with him, I would have to leave."

Shady nodded, then said, "Let's worry about that if Black Hawk comes to help. If they do, we will stand behind any decision you make, Moon. But it has to be yours."

We straightened the bathroom up and walked out when it hit me, and I stopped in my tracks. "We don't even know if they will come or if Creed will even call them."

"Uh... yeah... about that. You were already headed out of the room when it was agreed upon. They're calling them," Harmony said, smiled, and placed her arm over my shoulders.

"You know," Shady said as we walked out of the bathroom, "we need to have a serious discussion with the new Lady Riders. First Bob and now you. I mean, we have got to talk about protection, ladies. You know I love scaring the shit out of the men, but damn."

Chapter Five

Ghost

Most of the members were already at Soft Tails when I walked in. The place had been closed for the impromptu club meeting. This was my first official one as a full member. My heart felt light in my chest, instead of the heaviness that had weighed on me for so long. I knew who was to thank for the change, the men in the room. They'd accepted me into their fold, and it had started my healing without me even knowing, but the one who sealed the last crack in my heart had been Luna. She might be Moon to the Ops, but she'd never be to me. It would always be Luna.

I adjusted the crotch of my pants as I sat down in the back. The thought of being with Luna again had the same effect on me as it had when I'd turned sixteen. But the difference was before, it was just in my imagination. Now, with the night we'd spent together running rapidly through my mind, I closed my eyes. I could almost feel the softness of her wrapped around me. Every phone call I made to her, which was almost every night since we'd parted that morning, only sealed our fate more. It was time to figure out how we were going to make a long distance relationship work because to me, there was no other option. I'd lost track of her before over my stupid actions, but I wouldn't allow it to happen again.

Tank and Bull sat down beside me, and we waited for Crusher and the rest of the leadership to inform everyone why he'd called Church. No one had to wait long for the club's president to get down to business once the remaining few members had arrived.

"Going to lay it all out and then, if anyone has questions, you can ask them. Creed, the president of the Ops Warriors, called yesterday and they have a situation brewing in their territory. Their intel tells them the Black Hearts MC is gearing up to make a hit on their club. Most of you are familiar with the story about Jas and why she was sent here and put under our protection. Not only was she taken at an early age from her mother, but her life has also been under constant threat since. They know it's coming from Jas's grandmother; they just don't know why the woman wants to hurt not only her daughter, Shady, who's the leader of the Lady Riders, but her own grandchild, too. Well, other than she is batshit crazy by what Creed told me. Considering some of our backgrounds with our own relatives, we can relate.

"They think the Black Hearts not only want to take them out but have been promised if they do, the mining property the Ops had in Riverton, Nevada would be handed over to them. Not even going to get into the fact the Ops sold it to the Acciai family from Vegas. I'm going with the Black Hearts are a little short on brains if they think they can go up against the Costa Nostra and win. With that said, they have the numbers, though, to give the Warriors a run. So even with the help of the Furies, the Ops are going to be outnumbered. They would like to even that up—with our support.

"We've talked," Crusher waved his arm to Jag, Devil, and Flirt, who sat at the table with him and then pointed to Speed and Coast, who stood against opposite walls since they were club's enforcers and needed to see everything and everyone in the room. "We six are going. Stoker and the rest of the dads will fill in while we're gone. Keep in mind that enough need to stay here to protect our interests. Lending a hand is one thing, but I won't leave this club vulnerable in the process. Threat to us or not.

"Brothers, we won't know what we are walking into until we get there, so take that into account when you make your decision. Creed and his men from the Ops, along with Fling and his men from the Furies, and us would allow them the advantage with the Black Hearts. We would essentially bring the war to them."

Crusher went on the explain about the president of the Black Hearts, Sledge, and how he came to be in that position. When he finished, Stoker stood.

"Why would the six of you need to go? Don't get me wrong, I have no problem filling in, and I'm sure the rest don't either, but not seeing the reason for all the officers to go." Stoker addressed his son, and Crusher nodded.

"We understand the concerns for us going, but we can make use of this to also forge an alliance of sorts. The Ops still push guns, but other than that, they are much like us, ex-military, and working to clean up their club for the future generations. Besides, when has any club tolerated threats to women and children? I can't think of one." Crusher let that question hang and looked around the room at all the members.

I knew what my response was going to be. I'd been there when the call had come in.

"Count me in, Prez," I said and then saw the smile on Flirt's face. Bastard knew the deal between Luna and me.

"I'm in, too. I don't care what those fuckers think they're going to accomplish, and normally, I wouldn't give two shits. But Jas deserves to live without fear, and if wiping out some dumbasses with nothing but greed driving them, then they won't be missed," Dare said.

"Thanks, Dare. Creed asked me to tell you Trey's out. He's there, too," Crusher said, and Dare smiled.

Trey was Ops' way to pay back Black Hawk for watching over Jas. The club didn't know the entire story behind Trey, other than he was the son of Dare's youngest brother. The man died on a run, and the club whore he'd knocked up wouldn't let Dare and Shakes have any involvement with the boy.

Dare had kept track of them and knew the bitch had jumped clubs. When Trey had been just shy of his eighteenth birthday, the club used him as a scapegoat for a drug deal gone bad, thinking they'd go easy on him for his age and his first offense. Instead, the kid was tried as an adult and sent to prison for five years. But recently he was released on early parole after serving a little over three. However, he had to stay in the area as part of his parole.

"Appreciate it, Crusher. Shakes and I never expected you to use the Ops' marker to help Trey. But we won't forget the gesture. Ever."

"We told you why. Next to our dads, Shakes and you raised us. What we did doesn't even come close to what the two of you did for us growing up. So not another word about it." Dare nodded.

The meeting continued, and every man in the club agreed to give Ops their support. Since not all would be needed, Crusher lifted a paper off the table.

"The loyalty in this club has always held strong, and we knew everyone would step up, but like I said, we can't leave our own territory unprotected. I spoke with the others before Church, and we figured twenty would be enough to make the trip."

Crusher read the names that he and the other officers had made for the trip. Tank, Bull, Boss, Turk, Stem, and seven more were going to ride with Crusher, Jag, Devil, Flirt, Speed, Coast, Dare, and I.

"That is going a be a helluva trip to San Diego. You're going to need to take a truck and trailer to haul extra parts and shit with you in case something happens along the way. Be glad to do it. No sense in you young brothers riding in a cage." Roscoe looked at Crusher as he spoke and waited to see if Prez was going to nix his suggestion. Crusher gave nothing away in his expression as he looked down the table at the others, who shrugged.

Me and every man in the room knew what was probably going through their minds, and it had nothing to do with Roscoe's age. He was one of the oldest members of the club, but he was strong and could still handle himself one-on-one if need be. Nope, what was going through the officers' minds was did we want to turn the man loose on another club? With him along, the trip would be anything but dull.

"What the hell, it will be like taking granny from the *Beverly Hillbillies* into the city. But, Roscoe, those women aren't like ours. I have a feeling they just as easily chew you up and spit you out than put up with your shit."

"Ah, Prez. I ain't met a woman who didn't want a piece of Roscoe." The entire room erupted in laughter. "You fuckers are just jealous."

As we quieted, Crusher continued, "We pull out in two days, brothers. Meet at the compound, and we'll pack the trailer and truck and leave from there. We'll take two days to get there. It will be a long ass ride, but we need to be there like yesterday. The sooner we help the Ops dispose of their problem, the sooner we get home. And I mean all of us will come home. Got me?"

We agreed with our prez, loudly. Crusher raised his hand, and the room quieted.

"Since we're here, we have some other business to discuss. Was going to hold off on it until the next Church, but no sense waiting. I'm going to turn this over to our VP. Jag, the floor is yours."

"We know some of you have voiced that you wish there was a gym in town. We know a lot of you use the small weight room at the clubhouse. And some of you have your own setup in your house or garage. The building that houses Yoga Sensual is coming up open because the yoga place is moving."

I laughed when several of the brothers moaned.

"Don't get your panties in a wad, you pervs. They are only moving to the smaller section of the building. The big side has an open floor and would work great as a gym. If we open the membership to the locals, too, we think it could be very profitable. Especially after we spoke with Ghost about taking charge of it. He had a brilliant suggestion. Ghost, why don't you tell them about your idea for the place?" Jag looked in my direction when he spoke.

Yesterday, after Crusher finished with the phone call, we had finally gotten around to why they wanted me at the clubhouse. To say I was honored that they thought of me would be an understatement. But after we looked at the blueprints of the space, it hit me what else would work there.

Something the town didn't offer and with a gym next to it would work even better. I cleared my throat and stood.

"The space is large enough that it could actually be split into two sections with the construction of a wall, which would enable us to create two businesses instead of one. The gym would operate one side, and a massage parlor the other." I grinned at the 'hell yeses' that were shouted. "A *legitimate* massage parlor. The size of the space would allow for four rooms. We'd have to hire licensed masseuses, but don't see that being an enormous problem. The location of it with the gym would allow us to offer packages with the memberships. Add that a yoga studio would be on the other side, business should be good."

"You mean no extra paid services on top of the massage?" Tank asked, and I looked over at him.

"Not if we want it to stay open, considering the sheriff's department is half a block away." The men laughed, and when I sat, Flirt stood.

"I ran numbers on the gym side. Equipment, rent, membership fees, licenses. It would be more beneficial to buy the building for the long haul. I suggest we make an offer to purchase. We'll have the rent from the yoga place and if by chance the gym tanks, not like we can't put something else in there. As far as the massage parlor not making money, it will sustain itself. The gym side will start in the red because of the start-up cost with the equipment purchases, but if the membership takes off, it won't stay in the red long," Flirt said and then looked to Crusher.

"Then it looks as if we are going to have two more enterprises unless anyone has something to add or a reason we shouldn't go forward." When no one spoke, he continued. "We'll keep everyone updated on the progress. Now, Church is over, open the damn bar." Every member cheered. I had to agree. I definitely needed a drink.

After we put the chairs back in place, I moved to the bar and sat on a stool. Once my beer was set down in front of me, I tipped it up for a much needed drink. I was going to see Luna in four days. I wished it was under better circumstances, but no way would I let that damper my thoughts of seeing her again. Touching her, kissing her, holding her again.

"I know where your head is, brother," Flirt said and slapped me on the shoulder as he sat down beside me.

"Shit, is it that obvious?" I asked, while I stared at the bottle in front of me.

"Nah. Only to me because I know how you think," Flirt said, then took a drink of his own beer.

"True," was my only reply.

"Since we have been to hell and back together, Ghost, I'm just going to come out and say it. You want her, bring her back with you, man. Don't put it off," Flirt said, but never turned his head to look at me.

"She's been with the Ops and Lady Riders for a long time. They've been her family, Flirt. I just got her back in my life again. If I mess this up—"

"Might be, but I know you, Ghost. We've seen a lot, done a lot, and survived a lot together. I felt the loss of your

61

family with you. Then you came back here with me, and I've watched you grieve and barely living. I often wonder if the man I met when we went through BUD/S together and then onto the same SEAL team would ever surface again. In this last month, I've seen bits and pieces of him surface, and I believe it is owed to Luna. The old you went after what he wanted. Is that man back?" Flirt waited while I pondered on what he said.

"I'm back, but she's changed, Flirt. She's more than the young girl I let down." Flirt nodded and stood, and I looked up at him.

"So have you, brother. So have you," Flirt said, then turned to walk away, but he stopped and looked back at me. "She might be part of the Ops and the Lady Riders, and you both might have taken different roads for a while. But the way I look at it, Ghost—she's been yours a lot longer."

I sat there and watched my friend walk away, then I turned around and finished my beer. By the time I headed to my place to get my things together, the decision was made. When I came back to Shades Valley from San Diego, Luna would be with me. Even if I had to tie her to the back of my bike.

Chapter Six

Luna

Today was the day. I closed the door to my cabin and walked across the compound to the main building. When I walked in, Creed was disconnecting from a call, and the other men in the room waited to hear any new information he might have gotten.

Instead of interrupting by walking across the room, I leaned against the wall just inside the doorway to listen.

"Well, we aren't going to have to meet Black Hawk at the designated place with the trucks to bring them in undercover. The Black Hearts know they are here."

"How the fuck could they know that, Creed? We've been over every inch of this compound, checked the computer equipment, and scrubbed everyone's phones. They don't have shit of ours or the Furies bugged. Yesterday we caught the two that were sneaking around just outside both clubs' perimeters," Fork said.

"Those two are clueless to what they walked into. We hired them to watch us, and if we made any suspicious moves, they were to send a text to a number programmed into the disposal phones they were carrying. Data and Numbers ran that shit and surprise, it went to another disposal phone," Maxi informed everyone. From the expressions on the men's faces, none of them were happy.

"Yeah, and when I called it, no one picked up. All we have are two unconscious assholes in our shed who know jack shit about where the man that hired them is hold up," Ice said.

"The man found them in an alley where they live. They're just a couple of homeless men he walked up to and asked if they wanted to make some easy money. He was Native American, they said. I asked if he had a cut or vest on with the name Black Hearts on it. One guy didn't remember what the man was wearing because he was too busy counting the grand in cash he handed him, then he shoved each of them a disposable phone. He told them if they did well, they would pay the other four grand owed for their services. This was the interesting piece I got out of the other guy. He said he remembered the man had a leather vest on and when he turned to walk off, he noticed shit on the back. But the only thing he could recall was the first letter of each word. A D and an S in bold print," Maxi finished and waited. It didn't take long before the men clued in.

"Seriously? Sledge had his old club's vest on?" Creed asked, and Maxi nodded.

The room was quiet for just a second. I was sure they wouldn't appreciate if I said that shit took balls from Sledge, but it was damn impressive.

"The fucking shit gets more messed up by the damn day. When we think we're getting answers and close to piecing it all together, then more shit floats to the top," Fork said.

I couldn't have agreed more, and I'm sure I wasn't the only Lady Rider in the room that did. But we knew when to keep quiet.

"Only thing we can do is take care of one issue at a time. First up, Sledge and the other Black Hearts. And we need to do it sooner than later. That was Crusher I hung up with. They rode hard and were on the outskirts of San Diego when he called. Told them to come on in since we caught the ones watching us, so they should be here soon. Crusher said he had a little info for us when they get here, so after introductions, we'll have a meeting," Creed said, and he and the men headed out.

I moved off the wall and followed the other women outside. And as the door closed behind us, we could hear the faint sounds of pipes.

"I think company is coming, Pa," Kink said and laughed, drawing a glare from Creed.

With the sound of the bikes drawing closer, more Ops members gathered to greet the club. We watched from our spots in front of the main building as the motorcycles pulled up to the gate, followed by a Ford 3500 Diesel crew cab truck with a trailer attached. As the gate opened, the bikes filtered through until, finally, they reached our group. I ran my eyes over the men on the bikes as they were dropping their kickstands and dismounted. I spotted Brax. The man was hard to miss. When he stretched, my stomach flipped, and it had nothing to do with morning sickness.

"Holy shit! What the fuck do they feed those men in Washington?" Shady said, and her men turned to look at her.

"I know, right? I told you about Moon's man when we got back from picking up Jas. The other two with him that day weren't anything you'd kick to curb either," Harmony said, and I smiled when Creed and Fork moved beside her.

"He's not my man," was out of my mouth before I could control it, and Harmony turned her head toward me. All I could do was shrug.

"Right, like you didn't climb that tree and do some swinging."

"Harm, we are fucking standing right here," Fork said in a disgusted voice, and I was thankful for it because if Harmony was focused on Fork, it was off me.

"Moon, I think—"

"Freedom, I'd be cautious with what you think out loud," Easy said, and Freedom rolled her eyes at him. I used the distraction and stepped to the side with the hope they wouldn't notice.

"Not helping, Free," Poke said when Easy growled. Freedom turned to reply to Poke, but instead, grinned ear to ear with the other Lady Riders. I followed their line of sight and watched as an old biker stepped out of the truck and started toward us with the other men from Black Hawk.

"Well goddamn, they got some prime women in this club! You men sure these women aren't underage."

I would have laughed at the old guy if I hadn't felt the tension as the men moved until they had the women closed in between them as the group of men got closer.

"Aww, I like him. I always wanted a grandfather." At Shady's words, I watched a huge smile spread across the man's face, and I shook my head.

"Darlin', my thoughts are anything but grandfatherly."

Shady burst out laughing, and so did I and several of the other women. The men from both clubs, not so much. From Brax's reaction to wiping his hand down his face, I figured the behavior was typical of the older man.

"Fuck, Roscoe. Can you give us time to meet these men and their women before you start?"

I looked at the man who spoke and noticed he wore the president's patch. The old guy that he'd called Roscoe confirmed it.

"Sorry, Prez. Didn't mean nothing by it. I just said what the other brothers were thinking."

"Don't even bring us into your shit, Roscoe," was said by the man who stood next to him, and his comment had some of the Ops chuckling and becoming more relaxed.

Before anyone else could say anything, Jas came around the building and ran straight through the middle of us. She didn't stop until she was in the arms of the big man who had just spoken.

"Dare!" Jas yelled, and the big man held her up in the air and out in front of him with little to no effort. When the large man's name registered, I realized he was the uncle to Trey, the Ops' newest prospect.

I stopped hearing what everyone was saying around me when I looked back at Brax. He winked, then kept his eyes locked on me. Introductions were made, and he briefly looked away before he turned and headed in my direction. I opened my mouth to say hi but never got the chance to get it out. Brax grabbed me, wrapped me in his enormous arms, and covered my mouth with his. The kiss stole my breath and closed everything around us out. Being in his arms again felt like coming home.

When Brax broke the kiss and set me back on my feet, everyone from both clubs stood silently watching us. I'd never been easily embarrassed, but I felt the heat on my face.

"Well with that, Crusher, I think we should get you and your men squared away and then we can have a sit-down and get us all on the same page with what is going to go down. We also have a ton of food in the clubhouse kitchen to eat while we talk," Creed said.

"I agree. We haven't eaten since breakfast, and if I'm lucky, the food may keep Roscoe's mouth busy," Crusher answered.

"Aww, Prez. At least I didn't walk up and stick my tongue down one of the women's throat," Roscoe said and waved a hand in Brax and my direction.

"Roscoe, how has Sue not killed you in your sleep?" Brax asked, and the man's face broke out in a huge smile.

"Because I got what she likes, and I don't need a blue pill to help with it, either. I've told you boys that women love them some Roscoe."

I assumed from all the groans at Roscoe's words that the men from Black Hawk heard that frequently.

"Yep, I damn like him," Shady repeated.

"You would," Cajun said, and Shady elbowed him.

Before everything got out of hand, Creed and Crusher worked together, getting everyone moving. It wasn't the first time I noticed how everyone worked together as a unit. Sometimes it was easy for me to forget that the Ops' men had been in the military and Brax had told me the majority of Black Hawk men had been, too.

They proved it with the organized way everyone worked. It only took an hour, and everyone was back at the clubhouse eating. The women were allowed to attend the meeting if we swore not to interrupt, which left us sitting in the back of the large room while the men strategized on the best way to handle the Black Hearts.

"So, on your way in, you saw a few of them?" Creed asked.

"Yeah, we passed ten of the Black Hearts going the opposite direction on I5. We rode to the next exit, got off, and circled back around when we saw them take the exit ramp. By the time we did, they were nowhere to be seen. We drove around some of the area, passed a park called Petco or something like that. Not being familiar with the area, we weren't sure of any places around that would be big enough for them to stash bikes out of sight. I'm sure the president was with them because as we passed, he looked in our direction and he nodded his head. Got to say, strangest encounter I've ever had, and shit, after serving in Afghanistan and Iraq, my gut feeling has become the norm. And mine says Sledge wants you to find him," Crusher finished, and Creed sat back in his chair.

"Maybe the fucker wants to lure us to them because he knows our compound and the Furies is like a military armory. If they hit us on our turf, the outcome for them would be devastating. Could be they think we will leave just enough men here to cover, then they can send us on a wild goose chase and hit here," Fork added to the scenario.

"The area you're talking about is close to the Tenth Ave. Marine Terminal. It's roughly fifteen miles from the Mexico border, so that would be convenient for them if they needed to make a quick exit," Creed finally spoke.

"Could be they're in one of those warehouses the marina asked San Diego County to let them tear down. They're empty and not serving a purpose like the open space would. The marina could use it and be able to stack more containers," Boony said, and Creed looked at him and smiled. "What? I read the paper." A few of our men chuckled.

"Boony, you never fail to amaze me. Maxi, take a few guys and check it out. If it pans out, this shit could be easier than we expected. Especially if we plan a hit before daybreak. I will not get excited until we know for sure. But, damn, it would be nice to catch an f'n break." Everyone in the room agreed with Creed.

When Maxi stood, one of the men from Black Hawk stood, too. I looked at his patch and it read Enforcer.

"If it's alright with my prez, I'd like to go with you. I have a new gadget I'd like to try out," the man spoke to Maxi, but I noticed he looked at his prez for the okay.

"Works for me, Coast." Crusher looked toward Creed. I assumed to see if he had a problem with one of his men tagging along.

"Might not be a bad idea for several to go, Maxi. On the off chance, you run into a few of them while you're looking around," Creed said, and Maxi nodded in agreement.

Within ten minutes, six men rode out of the compound. Maxi, Easy, and Poke from the Ops and Coast, Tank, and Bull from Black Hawk. I was slowly learning their names, but what I noticed most was the interaction the men had with Brax earlier.

I'd thought then that he had landed in a good spot. He'd needed a place to heal from the loss of his family, and they'd given it to him. I'd even gotten to speak privately for a few minutes with Flirt. He'd been the one to convince Brax to go home with him after they left the SEALs.

When I focused back in from my thoughts and looked around at the men who were left, Flirt caught my eye and winked. I smiled at him and thought about what he'd said when I thanked him for helping Brax. His brief reply of *'That's what family does,'* meant everything to me and showed me just how much they cared for Brax.

While we waited for the ones who left to check in, the men talked about how to handle everything if they found the others at the marina. I only caught bits and pieces as the other women and I cleared plates and put the leftover food away.

I wanted to be alone with Brax, but I was thankful for the extra time to deal with the feelings that crept up on me when I saw him again. I also knew I needed to talk with him, though I wasn't in a hurry.

When we finished in the kitchen, we walked back into the main room and sat back down to catch more of the men's plan.

"So, we all agree. Furies stay and cover both compounds, and your club and mine go. If they are in the warehouses, we hit before dawn. Preferably around three a.m. Now, if the men would check in with some good news, we're set," Creed barely finished when his phone chimed. All conversation stopped as he read the text. When his head lifted and he smiled, the entire room relaxed.

"Sonofabitch, the assholes are in the warehouses," Fork said, and when Creed acknowledged with a nod, the room volume went up. Every man in the room threw out suggestions.

In all my time with the Ops, it had to be the first that none of the women spoke or even made one comment.

By the time the men hashed out a pretty solid plan, Maxi and the others walked in.

"Whatever plan you got, you're going to want to adjust it. Coast's toy is a beauty, and if it works as he says, this shit is going to be a fuck of a lot easier," Maxi said and looked around the room until his eyes landed on Data and Numbers. "Gonna need you guys to hook up a screen for us. Coast has the frequencies you need to tap into. If it works—we'll have eyes and ears on the Black Hearts."

"On it," Data said, and he and Numbers left the room. When they came back in, it was with a large screen and a laptop. We sat patiently while the men hooked it all together. Data's fingers flew across the keypad as Coast read off the frequencies and codes that would allow them to tap in. As the picture came up, the room fell silent as we looked at the screen filled with bikers. They sat or laid around in various spots of the warehouse as if they hadn't a care in the world.

"Okay, how the fuck did you guys get a visual on them with sound, no less?" Maxi smiled at Creed's question.

"Go ahead, Coast, tell them." Maxi chuckled.

"A remote-controlled car, specially designed with camera and mic encased. I took the remote apart and designed it to work with radio frequencies, giving it the ability to bounce from cell phone tower to cell phone tower, so it wouldn't lose a signal and stop in the middle of operating," Coast explained, then ended with, "I've got a couple more toys with me if we need them."

"Geez, sometimes, Coast, you scare me with the shit you come up with," Crusher said and chuckled.

"Oh, it gets better," Coast said and preceded to tell us how he drove the silent running car through the partially opened door to the warehouse. He only needed to get it in and to a spot out of sight. As he continued to explain, every set of eyes in the room watched the Black Hearts. Even on a screen, the confidence showed in the men. They weren't the least bit worried about being found.

Coast kept moving the camera around, and I finally realized why. He was searching for Sledge. And as I watched the picture change with different bikers, none had been Sledge.

I knew the plan was going to start an argument. I looked over at my friends, and I saw the set expressions on Harmony's, Freedom's and Shady's faces. It hadn't taken long, and the bitching began. The new plan made it safe for them to go now. But I couldn't remember a time I'd seen absolute resolve in the men's eyes. I even found myself a little disappointed about not being able to go. And with the 'no' that followed out of each of their men's mouths, I knew their ears were going to bleed after Harmony, Freedom, and Shady got done with them.

"Well, we are set. Everyone be ready to roll out at two-thirty in the morning. The Furies will be here around two to take their posts. I think we should get some rest before we pull out. It could end up as easy as taking candy from a baby, but anything can go wrong. We still need to be prepared for that," Creed said and stood.

"In agreement with you. I know my men could use a little shuteye before we head to the marina," Crusher said.

The room started to clear out, everyone going their separate ways. I'd planned to stay seated until the last of the men left.

"Come on, baby, let's go to your place," Brax said as he walked up and held out a hand for me to take.

I looked at his hand, then up into his eyes. The boy had turned into quite a man. The past was the past. I could no longer live in it any more than he could. I placed my hand in his. He pulled me up, and we walked out.

Time, it seemed, I was officially out of it. Hours had passed with everyone, including me, focused on what the clubs were going to have to do. It left me no time to think about my dilemma.

Now, as I walked beside Brax, it was the only thing that raced through my mind.

Chapter Seven

Ghost

Luna closed the door to her place, and when she turned around, I stood in front of her. From the moment I spotted her when I dismounted my bike, I wanted her. Everything about her had always appealed to me. When I married Stormy, I pushed the earlier feelings I had had for Luna into a nice, tidy box in my head. But once I saw her again, the sight of her blew the lid right off. As I looked down at her now, I knew Flirt was right. She might be a part of the Ops Warrior MC, but she had always been mine.

I pushed her back against the door, bent, and covered her mouth with mine. When I broke the kiss, it was only long enough to pull her shirt over her head, then my lips were back on Luna's. My Luna. I found the hooks with my hand and her bra followed next. Her pants were more of an issue, which caused me to break the kiss and step back to push them all the way down. I removed Luna's boots, and I not only relieved her of the pants but her thong, too. There was something to be said about a woman naked while a man stayed completely dressed.

Standing back up, I looked down at Luna, and her expression was one I would forever remember. Shock, but when I looked into her eyes, a whole different emotion floated in their depth. Desire.

"Luna, you are as close to perfection as a woman can get."

Luna said nothing. She just reached up and placed a hand on each of my cheeks, then went up on her tiptoes and closed the space between us until our lips met. She started the kiss, but I took over and devoured her. It was the only word to describe my demanding and thoroughly dominating kiss. One that would leave us breathless when it ended. I wasn't able to get enough of her. Our tongues dueled, and I ran my hands over Luna until I settled them on her hips. Each area of skin I touched left her with goosebumps.

I slid my hands behind Luna and grabbed the cheeks of her ass. I squeezed and caressed until the need for her was too powerful to fight. When I lifted her, she wrapped her legs around my waist, bringing her bare pussy in contact with the material of my jeans. Luna shifted to gain a better grip with her legs, and it placed her center in direct contact with my hardened cock. She rolled her hips, and I groaned and broke the kiss. There was nothing more I wanted than to sink into her heat. The thought had my cock throbbing. With the smallest of adjustments, I held Luna with one arm, and the other moved between us to unzip my pants.

Once I had the zipper down, my cock sprang free and I slipped it between Luna's legs. Rubbing my cock back and forth, letting her wetness coat my dick. She moaned and squeezed my length between her legs.

"Tell me you're ready for this," I gritted out between my teeth.

"Yes, take me," Luna whispered, then gasped when I dipped my head and bit her lower lip. My tongue laved over the spot to lessen the sting.

"Did you miss me, Luna?" I asked and rocked my hips, sliding my cock back and forth. The friction had Luna's head leaning back until it rested against the door.

"Please, Brax," she moaned when I pressed the head of my cock against her clit. She rotated her hips, and more moisture soaked my dick.

I leaned in and whispered in her ear, "You're so wet for me, baby," and the only thing Luna could do was nod. "So, so wet that my dick is slick with your juices. I don't know what I want more, to fuck you or lay you down, spread you wide, and put my mouth on you to get a taste."

Luna became wetter with each word I said. She shivered and rocked her hips.

"Either I just... I just need to come," she panted out, and I sucked her earlobe into my mouth, then let go and swirled my tongue around the outline of her ear.

"My woman's pussy is greedy. I can feel it trying to suck my dick in. I like that. So I guess you're going to have to wait for my mouth, baby, because I can't wait to feel your pussy stretched around my cock." I paused and raised my head. "Shit, I gotta grab a condom." I reached for my wallet, and Luna stopped me when she grabbed my arm.

"Don't! Just fuck me. I need to feel you. Just you."

"You sure?"

"Yes, I'm sure. Dammit, Brax, fuck me!"

I pushed the head of my cock to her entrance, and with one thrust of my hips, I pushed into the hilt. Luna's back arched, and I held still long enough to allow her to adjust to my size and then I pulled out and pushed in again.

Luna rolled her hips and flexed, tightening her pussy around me. My hands gripped her hard enough that there would surely be bruises, but I wasn't able to loosen my grip.

"You fit like a fucking glove and with the warmth and you being so wet for me. Goddamn, your pussy was made for me, Luna."

Luna moaned, and I picked up speed. I began pulling her down as I pushed up. As I continued to pound into her, the only things that were heard in the room were her moans, my groans, and the slapping of skin each time Luna's body made contact with the door.

"I'm so close!" Luna yelled.

"Me too, baby. Come on, take us over the edge."

She laid her forehead on my shoulder as I reached one of my hands between us and rubbed Luna's swollen clit, matching the speed with my thrusts. When I pinched her clit

Ghost (Black Hawk MC 4)

between my fingers, she bit my shoulder through my t-shirt, and I slammed into her one last time. My cock twitched inside her, and then I filled her with my seed while her body shook with her own climax.

There was no way to tell how much time passed as we let our breaths level out. Luna was the first to move and raised her head to look at me.

"Really?" I smiled at her question, knowing exactly what she asked.

"What can I say? It's been a long ass month and I couldn't wait any longer. Where's the bedroom, Luna? That was a warm-up. I'm far from being done." I pulled back, only to thrust my once again hardening cock back inside her.

Luna pointed, and I turned and headed toward her bedroom. As we reached the door, she tensed in my arms.

"Put me down!"

"I will when I get to the bed." I took a few more steps and wondered at the change in her. Luna began to wiggle in my arms.

"Now, Brax. Now!" At the panic in her voice, I lifted her off my dick and set her down gently. Luna wasted no time when her feet hit the floor. She took off at a run out the door.

I tucked my dick back into my pants and headed out of the room to follow her. When I reached the bathroom door, it was to watch her throw up the lid of the toilet and drop to her knees. I moved into the room and stood beside her and ran my hand over her head with one hand and rubbed her back with my other while she gagged and heaved into the bowl. I never said a word. I let her finish, then I moved and grabbed a towel, wetting it for her. Luna stood and wiped her face and then stepped to the sink. I watched her brush her teeth while I stood behind her, unable to bring myself to speak. When Luna was finished, she stood and looked at me in the mirror instead of turning.

Silence filled the air while both of us stared at each other. Minutes went by before I found my voice.

"How long have you known?" I finally spoke, and the tone was low.

"Suspected it a couple weeks ago, then the vomiting was my confirmation." Luna kept her eyes locked on me, and I acknowledged her answer with a nod.

"Were you planning to tell me?"

"Yes, as soon as you came into my cabin, but you didn't give me much of a chance."

"Good."

"I'm sorry," Luna whispered, and her eyes filled.

I had a hard time imagining why she was sorry. That feeling was so far off from what was going through me.

"Why the fuck are you apologizing?" I asked and reached for her and turned her to face me.

Luna looked up at me, "I just—"

No fucking way could she have thought I wouldn't want the baby.

I wrapped her in my arms. "Fuck, Luna. I'm the one who's sorry. You thought I was thinking of what happened with Stormy? It never entered my mind. I might have blamed myself for a while after losing her and BJ. And fuck, I can admit to even being lost for a bit, Luna. And to be honest, I still have days. But then I found you again, and now this." I moved her until I held her enough away from me to span my large hand across her middle. Christ, she carried my child. "I get a second chance. You're giving me that. And I won't lose it again."

There was no chance for her to reply before I had her in my arms and was headed back into her bedroom.

"Well, at least I will not have to fight with you to get you to Black Hawk," I said and released her until she stood in front of me.

"Fight to get me to Black Hawk?" Luna placed her hands on her hips and glared up at me.

"Oh, I was taking you back with me. He or she just made it easier." I pointed at her stomach and then started removing my boots.

"Hold on a damn minute!"

"Are you going to be sick again?" I asked as I bent and pulled off my jeans, leaving me naked.

"No," Luna said, but her eyes roamed over my body. Then her tongue darted out, and she licked her lips, and I went instantly hard.

"Keep doing that, and neither of us is going to get a damn bit of rest," I smirked when her head snapped up, and the look of guilt crossed her face at being caught ogling me. Then it changed. Luna's eyes narrowed and her brows drew together.

"You can't just strip while we are fighting!"

God, she was beautiful. Pregnant with my kid and a little pissed at me. I couldn't have loved her more. And I wanted nothing more than to show her by sinking into her so deep that it took her breath. The only thing that kept from doing it was the slight paleness in her face and the fact I had a job to do in a few hours.

"We aren't fighting. And why can't I be naked? You are." She looked down at herself as if she had forgotten that I stripped her at the door. "Now let's get in bed. I need a couple hours of sleep if I'm going to be worth a shit later. We left the hotel before daybreak and rode hard to get here. Plus, you need to rest, too. You're going to need your energy for when I wake up." I moved and pulled the covers down and laid down on her bed.

"Yes, we are!"

"No, we aren't. It takes two people to fight. You're going to have to wait eight more months and then you can fight with either her or him for sealing your fate if you want to be mad. When I leave here, you will be with me. Now, get in bed."

Luna stood there with her mouth wide open, and I lifted the covers up and waited.

"Braxton Samuel Carver, you are an asshole," she said and glared at me.

"Luna Wildflower Madison, I always have been. You just never called me on it," I said, then smiled widely.

"Oh my God, I can't believe I'm doing this," she said more to herself. She moved around to the other side of the bed and slipped under the covers with her back to me.

I released the blankets and pulled her into my chest.

"This kid better not have your damn smile," Luna said. I closed my eyes and pulled her closer without replying.

It was quiet, and I started to dose when she said, "Maybe it is that easy."

I smiled widely then and fell into the deepest sleep I'd had in a very long time.

Chapter Eight

Ghost

We rode through the streets and made our way to the Tenth Ave. Marine Terminal. With the number of bikes, plus the time of the morning, we'd left in intervals of four, five minutes apart, in the hopes of not to draw too much attention as a vast group would.

Some of us took the interstate, while others took the back roads. We'd planned to stash our bikes well before we reached the warehouse where the Black Hearts were hiding.

Arial shots that Data downloaded had shown a dirt service road that ran from a locked gate only accessed when the utility companies needed to work in the area. It was how Maxi and the others had snuck in before. So, it was where we planned to enter also, because no way would we be able to access through the main entrance.

My group consisted of me, Flirt, Maxi, and Ice. By the time we reached the entrance, the gate was open, and it looked as if everything was going as planned. We moved down the road until we reached the area we'd chosen from the map. It was spacious and would allow ample room to park our bikes. Then we would be on foot the rest of the way. The ones that left before us had their bikes positioned for a fast retreat.

Going in, time wasn't limited, but once the job was done, we timed our departure and distance from the area down to the minutes it would take responders to get to the scene. Especially with the short amount of time the alarms could be blocked. However, the noise, there was no way to muffle it.

My group joined the others to wait for the rest of the groups. No one talked and wouldn't until the business was taken care of. Hand signals would handle all communications.

Once the last men arrived, the mile hike to the backside of the warehouse took us six point seven minutes at the pace set by Speed and Easy. I rubbed my chest, thankful for not letting my workouts go by the wayside after I left the military.

When Easy's arm went up with his hand in a fist, we stopped. Coast prepared and launched one of his toys. The drone went up in the air and would circle the area around the warehouse, giving us a view of any possible activity. As we watched the screen, Easy let the signals fly. Two fingers meant two sentries were posted on the outside of the building. He motioned one was on the left side and one was on the right. The spinning finger let us know they were in motion, not stationary guards.

Flirt, Maxi, Ice, and I were up first. The sentries belonged to us. While we moved in, Data and Numbers monitored their computers and stood by to stop all alerts from reaching the outside. The four of us split when we were close to the warehouse. Flirt and I moved with no sound toward our mark. We were on our man in a blink of the eye, but the man didn't go down without a fight. He swung at Flirt. Flirt's hand flew out and throated the man. The only sound was the small, strangled breaths that the man tried to pull in before everything went silent.

"The others should be in position," Flirt whispered, and I nodded. I looked around and spotted some men as they moved in the shadows.

Flirt and I moved to the corner of the warehouse, and I grinned when the two remote control tanks headed for the metal door that was lifted approximately a foot off the ground. The gap was plenty enough space for the miniature tanks to roll under.

No sooner than we watched them disappear, the door came up, and a few bikers stepped out. I glimpsed the surprise on their faces before they shouted a warning, and then the sounds inside of men moving around and yelling filled the air.

"Fucking hell!" I yelled and moved out into the open as a biker started toward me. I drew my arm back, bent the fingers down on my hand, then punched forward and hit the man on his nose with the bottom of my palm. The move sent the bone in his nose up into his brain, and he dropped to the ground.

"Hope Data and Numbers have everything blocked because shit is going to get real," Flirt said as he and I took off for a row of stacked shipping containers about a hundred feet away.

Just as Maxi and Ice joined us, someone in the distance yelled, "It's a go!"

From our position, we watched the men take off for cover. The ground shook, and debris shot into the air. Then the sounds of it hitting the ground and pinging off metal rippled around us. When I moved to the edge of the container I was behind and looked out, the building was in shambles. The gigantic cloud of dust broke apart enough to show the building had been leveled. Coast's C-4 that he'd rigged on the remote control tanks had done its job. If anyone had a heartbeat under that rubble, they wouldn't for long.

Once the debris had finished falling, everyone moved from where they'd taken cover.

"Thank fuck the power and gas were turned off in the old ass building or this would have gone a whole other way," Creed said as we moved toward the building.

"We have fifteen minutes max to get the hell out of here and back to the bikes or we are going to have a lot to answer for," Crusher said as he walked up.

"If anyone is alive, the cops can deal with them," Creed said just as his phone went off. Creed pulled it out and read the text. "Goddammit, Sledge wasn't in the building. Data said when the men started moving around inside, there was no fucking sign of him. Where the fucking hell is he?" Creed shoved the phone back in his pocket.

"Fuck, Creed, we don't have time to worry about that," Fork said as he joined us.

"Yeah, I know. Pisses me the fuck off. Bug out, we are down to twelve," Creed said, and we started in the direction where we had entered. We reached the last row of shipping containers that looked to have been the last worked on for the day. Several were still stacked while a couple was in the air, held by the chains that would swing them onto a ship. I'd seen that plenty when our SEAL team would hitch a ride on a Navy vessel. The ship supplies were swung onto the deck by a crane, though they were crates instead of huge metal containers.

I was bringing up the rear when a man stepped out from between two containers. With his eyes on Creed, I tucked myself out of view on the other end of the container where the man had stepped out. As I moved around between the stacks to get closer to him, I heard the man speak.

"Looking for me, boys?"

I moved into position and as I stepped toward him, he never turned. His response was my acknowledgment that he knew I was there.

"Wouldn't do that if I were you. They're going to want to hear what I have to say, and by my calculations, this place will swarm with uniforms of all kinds in under ten."

Creed waved me off, but never took his eyes off Sledge.

"What the fuck, Sledge? You piece of shit traitor. You sold out your club for money. You—" Creed was yelling as he stepped toward the man.

"You don't know shit! Listen to me. I'm the least of your fucking problems!"

Creed stopped his advance.

"Fucking talk and then I'll decide if you live or not." Sledge chuckled at Creed's words.

"That won't be left to you, Creed."

"Fuck this shit," Maxi said and started to move.

'Stop, Maxi," Creed said, and Maxi stopped next to him. "Sledge, you got three minutes, so get to talking."

"Don't doubt her reach or her level of crazy. It has eaten at that bitch. We are nothing but her puppets. I tried to protect everyone and look where I am standing. I did what she wanted because my sister's kids were being followed. She told me wouldn't it be a shame if my brother in the military had an accident or Abi met her match in the ring. I raised them, Creed. They are my fucking blood, I couldn't chance she wouldn't follow through. I thought I was the only one she was working, but then I noticed Raven was drinking more than normal. Then he moved to drugs. She got to him and used his loyalty to you against him, along with his association with us. He never stood a damn chance. You do not know the way she fucked with his head, man, none. I used the Black Hearts to force my club out of town. I needed them gone if I was going to go against her. However, Raven and I weren't the only ones. She got wind of me trying to get Raven clean and contacted Heaven and Gage to tell them with their help, she would leave Raven alone, but if they didn't help her get me, not only would she hurt Raven, but Heaven's sister also would be taken and sold, again.

"By the time I uncovered that plot, Heaven and Gage had come back, and her flunky had killed them before he was taken out. Their bodies were placed in those tunnels with the other dead. Tell Raven I'm sorry. I failed him and everyone in my club. Don't play her game, Creed. You can't win that way. I know you're wondering how I could stay one step ahead of you. It was her. I knew Black Hawk would help you because she sent a man to see if Jas was there. When I found out he went without telling me, I killed him when he got back. The bitch knew Ghost and Moon grew up together before the two of them even knew where each other was." As Sledge continued, I heard sirens in the distance.

The Ops had explained the shit that had plagued them, but I hadn't understood the depth of it all until now.

"Come with us. Explain it all. We'll call the others and talk with them," Creed said.

"Go, Creed. I'm a dead man any way you look at it. Help Raven heal. If you can find my family, tell them I tried my best for them. But you need to leave now. I'll buy you some time to get as far away as possible." Sledge pointed toward the area where most of us had entered. "Go, I got this. It's the least I can do. But promise me you'll stop that crazy bitch!"

"We'll get her. But don't go out like this," Creed tried one more time before the sound of the sirens grew louder.

"No, go. Now!" Sledge yelled.

"Dammit, bug out!" Creed yelled.

"Move it," Crusher yelled, and I glanced briefly at the man as I passed him before picking up the pace.

We were at a full run as the first cop car turned down the row. We knew we had made it when we heard the squeal of their tires as the cars were brought to a stop. They would be too focused on the crumbled building and Sledge before they regrouped and searched the surrounding area. As we ran, I heard "Don't move!" Then the small tremble of the ground followed by the sound of metal hitting the ground. No one stopped or faltered in our steps. We knew what Sledge had done. He released the cable that held the containers in the air.

Fuck, what a way to take your ass out.

Once we made it to our bikes, it didn't take us long to clear the gate. Easy and Speed stopped and secured it back while the rest of us separated and took different routes back to the compound.

When we pulled through the gates, the sun was cresting, and the day showed signs it was going to be sunny. But our moods as we parked and dismounted our bikes was far from cheerful.

Chapter Nine

Luna

I opened the door and looked around the room while I pulled Brax inside with me. The party had been going on for hours. Creed had made all the calls they needed to with the information Sledge had given them. Shady's mother was going to be difficult. The woman had planned so much against the club; I couldn't imagine her going down easy.

When the men made it back, and Brax dismounted, I breathed a sigh of relief. That morning he'd woken me up just like he said and then left me warm and exhausted in bed.

The worry I had for him and the others was over. They'd come back, every one of them, and after taking care of a few things, it was time to party. There was a lot to celebrate. As we walked through the room, the booze was flowing, music was playing, and everyone was having a good time.

Well, the legal age people were having a good time.

"Just one freaking drink," Jas snapped at Cajun, who laughed and grabbed the bottle of beer from his daughter. It was good to see her adjusted to being back home.

"I don't think so, your mother would have a cow," Cajun said, and then Slider came up to Jas's side and flung an arm around her.

"I told you, I would be your favorite dad, right?"

I watched as she looked up at him and she grinned when he handed her his beer, and she took a drink.

"Thank you, Daddy!"

Cajun frowned, "So not fucking cool."

Brax chuckled as we moved away, but we could still hear Jas and her dads talking. When I glanced up at him, he smiled. "She is going to put those men through hell."

"They will gripe and bitch, but they will enjoy every minute," I said and grabbed a water and handed a beer to Brax.

"I can't believe you are really leaving us," Rain sniffed and hugged me when she and the other women walked up.

"It will not be forever. We can visit and stuff," I said softly, and Rain leaned back and glared at me.

"Damn right," Rain snapped and then stepped back and let Harmony have her turn.

"We are going to put the Black Hawk compound on our list of places to ride when we need a fucking vacation from all this shit," Harmony said, and when Brax coughed loudly, I whipped my head up to glare at him.

"What?"

"Nothing," Brax said, and Freedom moved closer to him.

"Better be nothing. You don't know what this woman means to us. So... you better know right now, when we call, and we will, she had better be happy and fucking spouting rainbows, or we are gonna let Shady loose on you."

I watched Brax as he looked around the room. Typical man searching for his way out when cornered in the middle of a group of women, where tears were a huge possibility.

Shady smirked, then whispered, "Here at the Ops, our men know when to rein us in and when to get the hell out of our way. Now is the time to get the hell out of our way, Ghost."

Brax stared back at Shady, then turned to me and leaned over and kissed the top of my head. "To show you just how smart I am. I'm going to go find Speed and the others and leave you women to it," he said, and I looked at him and smiled.

"No problem. Just come back here when you're ready."

Brax looked at Shay and the others and shook his head.

"No, baby, how about you come find me? You know? In case we get busy talking."

I shrugged and winked. "Not a problem. Go have fun with the boys."

As he walked away, I waited until the door shut before I laughed and turned to my friends. "Was that really necessary?"

Shady grinned and said, "Fuck yeah, it was. Next, we're going to send out Boo with a bloody knife to tell the guys the sacrifice is over."

We all laughed, and Harmony said, "You know, there was a time when we wouldn't have had the nerve to fuck with these types of men."

I looked around, "Yeah, but look around, without these men, we would be sad and lonely spinsters." They all laughed and then I continued. "Seriously, though, I'm not sure what the fuck I would have done without you guys. I mean, you are my family, all of you, and thinking about you not being there for the birth of my child...it sucks."

The women who had been my friends and as close as sisters stared at me. Freedom was the first to cry, and once the others noticed, they started, too. Soon, we were in a circle blubbering about missing each other.

We heard the door open, but none of us turned until we heard Roscoe's voice, "What the fuck are you all crying about?"

Shady wiped her eyes and looked at the older man and said, "Moon is leaving."

"Well yeah, I know that, darlin'. I was in her cabin with all of you, helping to pack her shit," he said, and when we just stared at him. He finally asked, "AND?"

Harmony frowned. "That is it, Moon is leaving."

"Honey," Roscoe said gently as he moved forward, looking at me. "You dying and not telling us about it?"

I shook my head and said, "Of course not."

Roscoe looked at us and shook his head. "Then there is no reason for you to be crying. She is not leaving, leaving, she is just moving her shit to another space."

"But we won't be able to raise our kids together like we planned," I yelled, and when Roscoe opened his arms wide, I threw myself into them. He wrapped his arms around me and patted my back.

Stupid hormones.

"Listen to ole Roscoe, honey. Once you are family, you are always family, and if you want something bad enough, well then, we will work this shit out. Because there is nothing more important than you women being happy," Roscoe said, which set the entire group of us crying again, but this time we at least smiled through the tears. When Roscoe let me go, the others took turns and hugged the older man.

This went on for a few minutes. When we were done, Roscoe nodded and said, "You all feeling better now?"

Shady sniffed and nodded. "Thanks, Roscoe."

"Anytime, sweetheart," he said, and then turned and walked out the door. When it closed, Shady turned to me.

"Damn, you are so lucky. I wish we had a Roscoe here, it would help teach the rest of these assholes how to behave."

The women continued to talk and as I listened, I thought about how much I would miss them. But then I thought of Brax leaving without me, and I knew my decision to be with him and to make the move was the right one. He was my future.

Hours later, as I laid beside Brax and caught my breath, I realized that wherever he was would always be home to me. Whether San Diego or Shades Valley, it made no difference.

"I can hear the gears in your head working. Second thoughts about moving to Black Hawk with me, baby?" Brax asked as he rolled me on top of him.

"No. I know it's the right decision. You're there, which makes it where I need to be."

"Dammit, I was going to let you sleep because we have a long fucking ride ahead of us, but then you say shit like that, woman, and all I want to do is sink into you," Brax said, and I felt the truth of his words hardening between us. I moved to straddle him.

"Yes, and I love your recovery time," I said as I slid back and forth, rubbing the length of his cock between my legs. He groaned, and I lifted, then brought myself down until he filled me. I moaned and rolled my hips, grinding down on him.

I threw my head back when Brax's hands moved to my breasts, and he started tweaking my nipples until they peaked. When I started to move again, Ghost stopped me by leaning up and replacing his fingers with his mouth. He took turns sucking and nibbling until I thought I couldn't take it much longer. But what I found was it was only the beginning.

Brax grabbed me by the arms and lifted me off his cock as he laid back on the mattress with me straddling his face.

"You probably are going to need to hold on to that headboard, baby. I decided I was a little hungry."

Before I had time to reply, I grabbed the rail with both hands as my knees buckled when Brax moved his hands between my legs, spread me wide open, and ran his tongue from back to front.

When he placed his focus on my clit, my head fell back, and the scream that came out of me echoed in the room. The orgasm caught me off guard and racked my body.

"Fuck, you taste good, baby. One more, give me one more and then I'll give you my dick," Brax said against my skin, then speared his tongue into my center and mimicked what he promised to do with his cock.

I squeezed my eyes closed and just felt. The second orgasm came on as fast as the first when Brax replaced his tongue with two fingers and sucked my clit into his mouth. He continued his ministrations until I came down. Before I could think coherently, I was on my knees with my face pressed against the mattress and Brax's cock at my entrance.

"Ready for me?" Brax asked.

"Fuck me, Braxton. I need you to fill me," I said breathlessly.

"That I can do," Brax said, and with the snap of his hips, he slid in to the hilt. I barely adjusted to the invasion when he moved. He pulled out, leaving only the head of his cock, then he slammed back in.

The room filled with heaving breathing and the sound of our skin slapping together as Brax took what he wanted from me.

I was confused when Brax stopped and pulled out, but it didn't last long because flipped me over and placed my legs over his forearms, opening me wide to him and then pushed back in. This time, he set a pace that had the headboard banging against the wall with each thrust of his hips.

"Eyes open, Luna. I want to see you go over with me," he said, and I opened my eyes to find his gray ones staring at me. Shit, I hadn't even noticed mine had been closed to begin with.

"One more, Luna. Give it to me," Brax demanded, but I wasn't sure I could. The man was riding me hard and straight into exhaustion.

"Just finish, I can't do it!" I yelled, and instead of fazing Brax, he picked the already fast pace up a notch.

"No way I'm going without you, so you can reach deep for it, or I will continue to fuck you until you do."

"I can't," I said and shook my head.

"You will!" he yelled, then reached with one of his hands and pinched my sensitive clit between his thumb and finger. With one last snap of his hips, Brax stilled, and I screamed through another release until my voice came out hoarse.

I laid with my eyes closed and listened to Brax move around. After he had cleaned me with a damp cloth, he tossed it somewhere in the room and laid down beside me. He pulled me until I laid with my back to his front, then he wrapped his arms securely around me.

"I love you, Luna. Thanks for giving me a second chance at life," Brax said, and I felt his chin as he rested it on the top of my head.

"Brax, I love you too. So much," I said, and then felt his lips as he kissed the top of my head.

Tomorrow would bring on a big change for us, but I was ready. I realized I may say goodbye to a chapter of my life, but I was starting a new one. As I settled and closed my eyes, I whispered to myself, "The adventure of a lifetime with my best friend."

Chapter Ten

Ghost

We pulled into the burger place's lot after we gassed up across the street. We'd ridden almost half the miles we planned for the day before we'd stop for the night. After we found a row of empty parking spots, we pulled the bikes in. With the spots in sight of the seating area, we'd be able to grab some food and keep them in view while we ate.

Luna held onto my shoulders while she swung her leg over and got off the bike. Once I kicked the stand down, I dismounted, too.

"You doing okay, baby?" I asked and placed my hand on her back and rubbed up and down after she shifted side to side.

"Yeah, just haven't ridden on a bitch seat in a while. Used to riding my bike. Better padding," she said as we watched Roscoe pass and head to the lot in the back where he could park the truck and trailer across two of them. Luna's bike was strapped down in the middle with a tarp secured over it.

"Sorry, baby. Didn't think of that. Only wanted you on my bike and snuggled up to me. Why don't you ride the next leg of the trip in the truck with Roscoe?" Luna smiled up at me, and I winked.

"Nothing to be sorry about. I enjoy holding onto you. And I'm fine. I'd rather be with you."

"Alright, but if you start feeling bad or get tired, let me know. We can stop, and you can swap and ride in the cage." Luna nodded, and with my hand on her back, I led her to the door behind the others. As I held the door open for her, Roscoe walked up and joined us as we entered.

Once inside, it wasn't long before everyone had gotten their food and sat at various tables and booths to eat.

"We'll stop for the night at the same motel we used on the way down. If they don't have enough vacancies, we'll keep going until we find somewhere else to stay," Crusher said from his seat at the end of the table.

"The rooms had double beds. Instead of two to a room, we could put four if they're short on rooms when we get there," Roscoe said from the table beside us.

"Speak for yourself. I'm not sharing a damn bed with any of you assholes. Bad enough sharing a room. Coast damn near sucked the fucking curtains off the window in the room we stayed in," Devil said, and we laughed when Coast punched his arm.

"I'm going to the restroom. Don't eat my fries why I'm gone," Luna said and pushed her seat back and stood.

"Now would I do that, baby?" I chuckled.

"Yes, and make sure none of the others do either. I've seen you guys eat. Everything gets inhaled."

At the 'hey we resent that' shouted around our table, she laughed and sauntered away.

"Bastards dropping like flies," Jag said and shook his head. I grinned at him.

"You jealous, VP?"

"Damn straight I am."

"Well, why don't you defrost the ice princess?" Flirt asked, and the entire table laughed when Jag flipped him off.

"The ice princess?" I asked, and Flirt snickered.

"The woman who bought Sami's house. Seemed she wasn't impressed with our VP's charm and good looks." Jag growled at Flirt, making him laugh louder.

"Come on, Flirt, don't you think you're being a little rough on Jag?" Coast said, then chuckled when Jag turned and glared at him.

"Bunch of assholes. Woman damn near ran me over, then when she spoke, I'm surprised I didn't get frostbite," Jag said, and picked up his burger. "Hell, seen her in town a few times since and when she notices me, she sneers."

"Are you talking about River? She was really nice to me when I had to go by and re-fix the window that was replaced after Prez shot through it," I said as Luna walked up.

"How nice to you?" she asked as she sat down.

"I don't notice other women, baby. I only see you." I winked and leaned over and kissed her forehead.

"You're so full of shit," Luna said, and laughed.

"Got your number, Ghost." Flirt put his arm around Luna, then laughed when I pushed his arm off.

"Let go of my woman."

"You're so easy to stir up." She chuckled and started eating her fries.

"Yes, I am. And when we reach the motel room later, I'll let you take full advantage of me."

"Eat your food."

"I would rather eat—" Luna's hand went over my mouth, cutting off my sentence and the others laughed.

"Hush, there are kids in here," she said, and my lips twitched behind her hand. "Behave." She dropped her hand and picked up her hamburger.

Everyone went back to eating, and the talk turned toward the rest of the trip. Where we'd stop. What the weather looked like ahead of us.

Luna listened and joked with my brothers as though she'd known them forever. I watched her laugh at something Roscoe said and then smile as Speed talked about Ally and the oil incident. They were all trying to make her feel comfortable, and I appreciated it.

When we loaded up that morning, and she'd said her last goodbyes, I wondered if I'd asked too much of her by giving up her friends to live several states away with me. But no way would I have her and my kid living any other place than with me. That was one thing I could control this time around. Before, the military controlled the places they sent me, and I'd spent a great deal of time away from Stormy and BJ because of it.

I smiled when Luna actually snorted at Devil's story about him, Neely, Jag, and I. Then he told her about how Devil had no clue about kids, but that he was catching on quick.

The only time I saw her smile falter was when my brothers mentioned their ol' ladies. I hadn't considered she might be nervous over meeting the women in the club.

"Well, if everyone's ready, let's ride. We aren't getting closer to home by sitting here," Crusher said and stood.

We stood and started clearing up our mess and tossing it into the trash. As we headed out the door, Roscoe held on to it while the rest of us stepped to the side to allow a group of women through the door.

"Ya want to ride with me for a while, darlin'? My rides bigger than his," Roscoe said and jerked his thumb at me. Luna shook her head and rolled her eyes at him while we waited for the ladies to pass.

"I got more than enough for her to handle," I replied to Roscoe just as the first woman walked in.

"I just bet you do, honey," was said by the woman, then she looked at Luna. "And aren't you one lucky lady," she said as she walked past, looking the brothers over as she went.

"Susan, you are going to get us in trouble one of these days," one of the other women said, and smiled. The woman they called Susan stopped and turned to her friend.

"Cathy, there isn't a woman breathing that wouldn't look forward to the trouble I bet these men offer." Susan waved her hand in our direction. The other women with Cathy and Susan giggled. "Look at girlfriend there," Susan pointed at Luna. "That smile she's wearing isn't because the sun is shining outside."

"Ma'am, I can be any kind of trouble ya want," Roscoe said, and Susan winked at him. "There might be snow on my roof, but there's enough fire below to keep you heated for days."

Everyone groaned, except Luna. She laughed and grabbed Roscoe's arm.

"Yep, time to go, grandpa," Luna said as she pulled Roscoe out the door.

"Told you women can't resist me," Roscoe said and threw his arm over Luna's shoulder.

"Jesus, his ego gets any bigger, he won't fit in the truck," Crusher said, then looked at the women. "You've made our day, ladies."

"Sweetie, I'd make your week if I wasn't married," Susan said, and Prez laughed and headed out the door.

"No doubt you could, ma'am. Enjoy your lunch," Jag said and winked before he followed Crusher out the door.

I held the door open while the others followed. And when the last of my brothers walked past, I let the door shut behind me.

Luna wasn't beside my bike and I looked across the parking lot and saw her with Roscoe, helping him check the tie-downs on the trailer.

"The man could use some meds," Flirt said as I approached my bike.

I laughed. "I'm not going to argue with you about that. But you've got to respect how he enjoys life with no apologies," I said, straddled my bike, and looked in Luna's direction. I smiled when she laughed at something Roscoe said, then started across the lot toward me.

"I need to worry about Roscoe stealing you from me," I said as Luna got closer.

"Not sure. Because he does have a big... truck," she said, and Flirt chuckled.

I flipped Flirt off and swatted Luna's ass as she passed me to get on the bike.

"My ride's smoother and has more power," I said and laughed as she pinched my side. Once she was on the back, I started my bike along with the others. As soon as Roscoe's truck started across the lot, we began pulling out. There were a lot more hours to ride before we stopped for the night.

Chapter Eleven

Luna

Who knew carrying a baby the size of a peanut would exhaust you? Certainly not me. What did I know about babies? Zip. Zilch.

My mind ran wilder with every mile we drove. The worry of being someone's mother. The worry of what the women of Black Hawk would be like. Would I fit in? The only thing I had no doubt about was Brax. I loved him even when I didn't know what the word meant.

The truck slowed and brought me out of my head. When I looked out the windshield, we were following the bikes down the exit ramp.

"You feel okay, sugar?" Roscoe asked and glanced over at me.

I'd been riding in the truck with him since we'd left the motel that morning. The first day, I spent on the back of Brax's bike. The second day, and now the third, was spent in the truck. Brax thought it was best since I spent the better part of each morning hugging the toilet, which was a new level of gross because of the whole thing about getting up close and personal in a motel's bathroom.

"Yeah, I feel a lot better."

"Good." Roscoe turned right at the end of the exit.

"Is this the exit to the club?"

"Nope, last gas stop. The bikes could've made it, but no sense in us rolling in on fumes. We've got about an hour left," Roscoe said while he maneuvered the truck and trailer into the station's lot and stopped beside one pump. "You getting tired of riding?"

"A little. And I want to thank you in case I forget to tell you when we arrive. You men have been great. I know you probably would have pushed to get home sooner, but..." I trailed off and grinned at Roscoe.

"Ah, darlin', we take care of our own. And make no mistake, you are ours now. You became ours the minute the munchkin took root. So, with morning sickness kicking your ass, we might not understand it, but it makes you feel bad, and that we can help ease. Even if it means taking some extra time to get home."

I felt my eyes fill, and I blinked to get rid of the tears.

"None of that. Besides, more time away will only make Sue miss me more, which means I'm gonna benefit big time." Roscoe wagged his eyebrows at me, and I couldn't help but laugh.

"If I were older, I would fight every woman for you, Roscoe."

"Ah, sugar, there's more than enough of me to go around." Roscoe opened his truck door as Brax opened mine.

"You got your own woman, Roscoe. Stop hitting on mine," Brax said over the cab of the truck.

"Aww, please. You boys are delusional, they are mine," Roscoe said, and started fueling the truck.

"What are you smiling about, baby?" Brax asked as he helped me out of the truck.

"That Roscoe is too cute," I said, then laughed when I looked up and saw Brax's face.

"Christ, don't say that where he can hear. The man's bad enough," Brax said, disgusted.

"Oh, sweetie, you're the only man for me." I laughed when Flirt walked past us and groaned.

"Pathetic, another brother down." I'd barely heard Flirt's mumbled words.

"Don't listen to him. He's just jealous," Brax said, and stopped us before we entered the store. When I looked up at him, he lowered his head and took my mouth with his. The kiss was brief, but as he broke it, he rested his forehead on mine. "Feel like riding the last bit with me? Miss your arms wrapped around me, baby."

Flirt was wrong. His brothers weren't the pathetic ones. It was the women for sure. How could their resistance ever hold against the men? Mine couldn't. As I stared into Brax's eyes, I knew then that he was the one with the power to destroy me because there was nothing I wouldn't do for or give to him as long as he continued to look at me like he was now.

"I feel great. I missed riding with you, too," I answered and kissed him.

"Hey, if you two can hold off. We've only got about an hour left," Crusher said as he stepped out the door.

"You got it, Prez," Brax said to Crusher, then walked me into the store. "I'll get us something to drink while you use the restroom."

I stared at Brax and didn't say a word.

"You don't have to go?" Brax asked, and grinned.

"Well... yes, I do. But you don't need to keep track."

"Not keeping track. Just hard to miss since you've gone every time we've stopped." Brax's lips twitched, and I huffed and turned to the back of the store where the restroom sign hung. He smacked my butt and laughed when I shot him a glare over my shoulder.

"Men. They think they know everything," I mumbled as I walked into the ladies' room and hurried into an empty stall.

By the time I took care of business, Brax had drinks in his hands with a package of crackers. I ate the crackers on the way to the bike, and after the rest of the men finished filling up their bikes, we were ready to hit the road for the last leg.

The end of the trip was over in no time, and before I knew it, we were taking the exit and then driving through town. Everything was just how Brax had described it to me in San Diego. But when we reached the cutoff to the club, not even his description did it justice.

The area was beautiful. We rode up the road and slowed as the gate came into view. Once the young prospect opened it, we continued through. As the clubhouse came into view, I noticed bikes parked off to the side, then as we got closer the door opened, and men stepped out. The group that gathered waited for us to stop.

I got off the bike and stood beside it and waited for Brax to dismount. When I heard the small voice yell "Daddy," I turned and watched a little girl barreling toward us with her black ponytail swinging as she ran.

"That's Speed's little girl, Ally," Brax said, and I smiled as I watched the big man catch her as she launched herself at him.

"Hey, where's my love?" Devil yelled beside us as he faced the group with his arms out and palms up.

I turned back to the group, and a smaller, light brown-haired girl was walking toward us. She looked dainty and sweet until I looked at her face. She wore a smirk that totally defied the rest of her little angel appearance. When she reached Devil, he squatted down and stuck out his hand and palmed her face, then picked her up and hugged her.

"That one is Neely. She Dev's sister," Brax said, then grabbed my hand and squeezed it. "You ready to meet everyone else here, baby?"

"Not sure there's a choice at this point," I said as we started toward the group of people.

Chapter Twelve

Ghost

After the welcome home hugs and kisses, it seemed everyone's attention immediately turned to Luna. I let go of her hand and draped my arm over her shoulders and pulled her into my side.

The trip had been long and tiring, and I wanted to take Luna home, but I knew that wouldn't happen until the club women got to meet her. If not here, there was no doubt they would converge on our place without a thought.

As we walked past the truck, some men were unloading the gear that we kept stored in the clubhouse.

"Hey, Ghost! After we get the truck and trailer unloaded, you want me to drive the trailer over to your place and drop the bike and Luna's stuff off there?" Roscoe asked as bags and supplies hit the ground.

"Thanks, Roscoe, that would be great."

"How far from here is your place?" Luna asked.

"First, it is our place. And it's in t—" I was cut off before I could explain that we'd have to go into town to the apartment.

"The cabin here is ready for you. After Russ called, we got busy, and we finished moving the rest of Roscoe's shit to Sue's house, then cleaned the cabin. A few of the men went to your apartment, Brax, and moved your things. All but your truck, it's still parked there. We didn't have time to clean your apartment either, which shouldn't take any time. You are one clean and neat man." Carly winked at Luna. "Trust me, it is a bonus. I've been inside a few of their places. Slobs and when you walk in, the first question you ask yourself is when you had your last tetanus shot?"

"Carly, darlin'?" Crusher said and shook his head, then looked at me. "Sorry, brother. My fault for mentioning you and Luna might take the cabin over once Roscoe finished moving his stuff out." Crusher looked down at Carly.

"What? We didn't have anything else to do while you guys were gone. You can't expect me to sit around looking pretty."

"For God's sakes, remember the whole you were shot and supposed to be taking it easy for your leg to heal?"

"I didn't say I moved the fucking furniture. That's what we used the guys for."

"The men have jobs and were supposed to be protecting the club while we were gone."

"It was after business hours, and they were protecting the club. It just happened to be while they moved some furniture. Are you admitting that men can't multitask?"

"What the fuck, Dad? You and the other dads were in charge while we were gone," Crusher looked back at his dad, Stroker, and asked.

"Yep, we were. Club is still here, isn't it? As for controlling your woman? Yeah, there aren't that many hours in a day." Stroker chuckled and walked up to Luna with the other dads.

Prez pinched the bridge of his nose and closed his eyes. As I looked around, the others were barely holding in their laughter, including me. When I looked down at Luna, her lips twitched as she watched the couple.

Some men chuckled as they passed by, carrying the things to the clubhouse, and Carly turned to glare at them.

"Welcome to the club, darlin'," Stroker, Preacher, Romeo, Cruz, and Flyboy said. I chuckled when a blush formed on Luna's face as they each took turns and bent and kissed her on the cheek. They might have caught my woman off guard, but I knew she'd recover quickly.

"Thank you. And just let me say damn. Older men have never done it for me, but you five could've changed that. If I didn't have Brax or weren't carrying his spawn, I'd be tempted to say spank me, Daddy."

The dads stared at Luna, and all the talking stopped, and the entire group went quiet. Flirt walked up beside Luna and reached around her back and slapped me on the shoulder. When I looked over at him, we both chuckled.

"Christ, Luna, I've never seen them speechless," Flirt said, but looked at his dad and smiled.

"No shit," came from Jag, Devil, Crusher, Coast, and Speed.

"We're gonna love having you around, darlin'. You're good for an old man's ego," Romeo said as the dads got over their initial shock.

"Hell, I wish I'd known you were looking for a... Daddy, because, sugar, you wouldn't have had to ask me twice to spank that fine ass."

I groaned and so did the others as Roscoe walked up and joined in.

"Yeah, because then we could be on a Jerry Springer episode. He's her grandpa and daddy," Luna shot back. It took a minute for everyone to figure it out, but then laughter broke out.

"Now that was just plain mean, darlin', to insinuate that I would not only sleep with my imaginary daughter, but that I'd knock her up," Roscoe answered.

"Oh, Roscoe, what would be mean is if I let you believe you could handle all this," Luna said and waved her hand down her body. I didn't know who she'd caught more off guard with the comeback, me, or Roscoe.

"For fuck's sake, why did you let her ride with Roscoe, Ghost? He has rubbed off on her," Flirt said, and the others laughed.

"Well, about time someone can put the man in his place. Glad to have you here, sweetheart. I'm Sue and the yahoo belongs to me." Sue hugged Luna, then looked at Roscoe. "You tease the girls too much. If they took you up on half the shit that comes out of your mouth, the club would hold a funeral," Sue said, and Roscoe threw his arm over her shoulders.

"Oh, Sue, you know I enjoy messing with them. But I save all this," Roscoe waved his hand to indicate his body like Luna had done, "just for you."

Luna turned her face to my chest, and I felt her body shake against mine as she laughed. She was relaxed around the club, and I was glad to see it. They were my family, and I wanted her to accept them as hers, too.

"On that note, I'd say we finish up the meet and greet. I'm Carly, and I'm sure you know I'm the better half of Crusher. And I love your bike and glad there is another woman who rides. I've been trying to talk these two into learning," Carly looked over at Sami and Bailey, then back to Luna, "but no luck."

"Hi! I'm Sami. Kane's ol' lady and Ally's ours. Please don't judge us by the crazy one. Kane didn't know he had a sister until recently." I grinned as Sami stepped in front of Luna, blocking Carly, who stared at the back of Sami's head when Sami thumbed over her shoulder to point at Carly. "She hasn't been cleared to go back to work or ride her bike, and she is going stir crazy. Not that she isn't normally a little... well, you'll learn. She's just overly stressed now."

"Yeah, and Sami is under the delusion that because she is pregnant, she is funny. Instead of bitchy and a pain in the ass." Luna laughed at Carly and stuck her hand out to Sami.

"Nice to meet you, Sami. And I can deal with crazy." Sami smiled at Luna and shook her hand.

"I'm Bailey, and Lance and Neely belong to me. I'm a nurse for Dr. Monroe. She is an OBGYN. When you're settled and are ready, tell me, and we will get you in to see Mac."

"Go ahead and set her up an appointment, Bay. She needs to get in there," I said and earned a glare. "You haven't seen a doctor yet. You need to."

"Yes, and I'm sure I could have answered Bailey without your help. Considering she was talking to me."

"Ooh, we are going to get along great." Carly clapped her hands, and I looked over at my prez.

"Sorry, brother. Too late, you've accepted the patch."

"Welcome to our hell," Speed said, and Sami turned her face up at him.

"Really?" Sami asked.

"I just meant because it's warm and cozy there," Speed said, and smiled when Sami rolled her eyes.

"Talk about pulling that save out your ass," Devil muttered, and Bailey elbowed him.

The other women stepped up and welcomed Luna. Shakes informed us both that if we needed anything, we only needed to come and knock on their door since she and Dare lived next to us.

"Except tonight," Dare said, and Shakes smacked his arm. "Darlin', I ain't been laid in a week. Once I close the door at our place, not opening until tomorrow. And might not do it then."

"Oh my God, Dare, there are little ears around," Shakes scolded and looked to where Ally and Neely were. Thank God, they were by the trailer with a few of the brothers, looking at Luna's bike.

"They aren't ours, so we don't have to do any explaining," Dare said and chuckled. "Besides, you act like we're going to be the only ones bouncing the headboard off the wall, sugar."

"Just a tip. The egg crate stuff people use to make their mattress softer. Cut two pieces the size of your headboard and staple one to the back of the headboard. The other, dip in the same paint color as your wall, then attach it with Velcro. Cheaper than fixing the wall all the time and cuts down on sound."

"Got any tips when people are plain ass loud?" Devil asked and looked at Crusher and Carly. It didn't take Luna long to realize what he was getting at, even though she hadn't heard about their first time in Crusher's house when they left the window open.

"Well, nothing short of a ball gag, really," she said with a straight face. Everyone looked at each other, then laughed, and Luna smiled.

"What am I going to do with you?" I asked.

"Take me home and love me."

I grinned, leaned down, and kissed the top of her head. I forgot how comfortable she always was around people and was glad she hadn't grown out of that. She laid her head against my arm.

"You tired?"

"A little and hungry."

"Brax, we stocked basic stuff, and some of the other ol' ladies made a few casseroles and set them in the fridge. Didn't think after the trip the two of you would want to go running to the grocery," Bailey said. "And I left you a little something on the kitchen island from my mom's bakery."

"Claire's strawberry cheesecake?" I asked and cocked my brow.

"Yes." Bailey winked.

"Umm... cheesecake?" Luna tilted her head up at me and smiled.

"Not just any cheesecake, the best cheesecake."

"Nice to meet everyone. Thanks for making me feel so welcome. Can't wait to get to know everyone better. But wherever that cheesecake is, I need to be there."

After a few more exchanges, I put Luna on the back of my bike, while Roscoe and a couple of brothers followed us to help unload her bike and things.

It hadn't escaped me that I'd probably smiled and laughed more today than I had in a very long time.

Chapter Thirteen

Luna

"Some cabin," I said as I stood by the bike and looked around the area. "It's beautiful here." I turned in a circle and took in the entire area. I could see at least six other cabins. Well, if you could call them that, randomly placed to give the residents some privacy.

"Flirt told me that after the club bought the property, they renovated the cabins and enlarged them. They didn't want to lose the rustic look, so they stayed true to that and built onto the original places. It took Stroker and the others a couple of years to get everything done, but they did. Then he and the other leadership lived in the houses on the other side. When Flirt and the guys started making their way back, they built themselves smaller places by the pond that sets toward the back of the property and turned the original houses over to their sons."

"Well, they did an awesome job because even though the cabins are more like houses, they still fit into the landscape. Are they all lived in?"

"Yeah, I think so. Most of the single guys live in town. The clubhouse has rooms upstairs, but they use those if someone gets drunk at a party and can't drive. Mostly the prospects use them when they're on gate duty. They can switch out and catch a few hours of sleep, but still be close if needed. I stayed in one of the rooms until I found a place in town. I had a one bedroom apartment. I didn't need much space for just me. Why don't you go inside, baby, and relax while I help the boys get your stuff carried in and your bike unloaded off the trailer?" Brax led me up the couple steps to the porch, then opened the door.

"Why would Roscoe want to move from here?" The room we walked in to was large, and everything was as rustic as the outside. Vaulted ceiling with the wooden rafters in view. A fireplace sat in the middle of the outer wall and was stone except for the mantle that matched the rest of the wood throughout the room. A few boxes were sitting against another wall, and a big ass TV was in the corner, sitting in what looked like a built-in bookcase slash entertainment stand. On one shelf sat two wooden boxes of similar size and color.

"Sue has a house in town, and Roscoe moved in with her. Most of the married members live in town, too." Brax walked me to the couch. "Sit, baby. Put your feet up. It won't take us long, then we can see what the ol' ladies left in the fridge. While the food is heating, we can look at the rest of the inside. I've only been here a couple times, and only downstairs when I was."

"Okay, sounds good." I sat on the plain brown couch that looked out of place in the room. Brax leaned down and kissed my forehead, then went back out the front door.

Besides the couch, there was an end table, a lamp, and a chair, but not much else. Brax and I would definitely need more furniture if this was where we were going to stay.

I pulled my boots off, then leaned my head back on the couch and curled my legs to one side. With my eyes closed, I listened as the guys came in and went back out, either after going up the steps or plopping what they carried on the floor in the room where I was. Their voices as they talked to one another must have lulled me to sleep because the next thing I knew, Brax sat beside me with my legs stretched across his lap as he rubbed my stocking covered feet.

"You're good at that." I raised my arms over my head, which was now resting on the arm of the couch, and stretched. "I didn't mean to fall asleep. How long was I out?"

"'Bout an hour and a half. You need the rest, baby. Come on, I put a taco casserole in the oven, and it should be done. Let's get you fed." Brax ran a hand up my leg and squeezed my thigh. "Your stomach was growling while you slept. I could hear it over your snoring." He lifted my legs and stood, then dropped them back to the couch.

"I do not snore." I sat up and glared at him, and he laughed.

"Baby, you do. And it's cute."

"There is nothing cute about snoring. And I don't so stop saying I do." I stood and started toward the kitchen with Brax laughing as he followed.

"Think I would know since I'm the one hearing it since you're asleep."

"Whatever," I said as I walked through the doorway to the kitchen and stopped.

Though the downstairs was open, the only view from the living room was the kitchen table. Which was square with only two chairs. Another thing that would have to be placed on my mental furnishings list.

"What's wrong, Luna?"

"This kitchen makes me wish I was a cook. Not that I can't whip up a meal, but this is meant for so much more." The double oven, to the stove, to the three-door fridge, all of which were stainless steel, went perfectly with the brown granite countertops, with matching backsplash.

"Well, sugar, you got all the time in the world to practice with new recipes." Brax moved around me and pulled the pan out of the oven and set it on the island that separated the eating area from the cooking side of the kitchen.

"Brax, I can't sit around every day with nothing to do. I'm going to need a job." I pulled out one of the bar stools and sat.

"Luna, I know we haven't talked about money. But I have plenty. Really more than enough. I invested what I inherited from my parents. I've got life insurance money from Stormy and BJ set back because I couldn't bring myself to deal with it. Using it didn't seem right. That's not including what I put into savings out of my military pay. And I make a decent living with what I earn as a stipend from the club, which will go up with me running the gym and the massage parlor." I watched Brax as he moved around the kitchen, locating dinnerware and utensils, then setting them on the island, too. "So, no need for you to work. Think of my money as our money, baby."

"Brax," I said with a sigh. "It's not about money. I need to work. I'm not the lying around type. I will go batty if I don't have something to do. It can be part-time or anything, really. Black Hawk has a strip club, right?"

Brax took the stool next to me, and I started serving the food. When he didn't respond, I looked over at him, and his jaw was clenched, and his nostrils were flared.

"What the hell has you mad? I didn't go off on a tirade when you were telling me you pretty much wanted me to stay home and cook."

"You might've worked at the fucking strip club at Ops, but I'll be goddamned if you work at Soft Tails. My ol' lady ain't taking her fucking clothes off for no one again, but me."

I laughed, which wasn't the right response because Brax stood abruptly, and the stool tipped over and hit the floor by the force. He stomped to the fridge and yanked the door open.

"Water or soda?" he bit out, and I stifled my laughter to answer. He slammed the can of soda down in front of me and a beer beside his plate before he bent and picked the stool up, then sat back down. "Laugh all the fuck you want. But you won't be stripping here. That's fucking final."

"Are you done ordering me around?" I asked as sweetly as I could without snapping at him. He'd misunderstood my question and jumped straight to the extreme.

"Probably not, but you'll have to get over it." He picked up his fork and started eating.

"Well, now that we have that worked out." I chuckled, and his head whipped toward me, and the vein at his temple was protruding. "Sweetie, I didn't mean I wanted a job stripping. But I know the business. And I'm not talking about the strippers. There's inventory of the bar and kitchen. Scheduling, you name it. I also know how to tend bar. And if there's nothing there I can help with, maybe one of the other club businesses could use some help."

"Just want time with you, baby. But I'll check for ya." Brax leaned over and kissed my forehead. "We can talk more about it later. Eat."

"So bossy," I said and picked up my fork and started eating.

"Yep," he said and smiled at me, not ashamed.

"Well, since you were so sweet about me letting me work," I said, then laughed when he looked over at me and smirked. "And you are even willing to share your money. I guess I could do the same."

"Luna, I will not use the money you make. You spend it however you want, baby."

"Umm... Brax. I'm not talking about a paycheck. I've invested well, too. The mine the Ops owned in Riverton brought in a shit ton of cash, then more after they sold the rights. Everyone got a share. My share was... three million and some change."

Brax had taken a bite when I said the amount and started to choke. I reached over and patted his back while he took a drink of his beer.

"Christ, woman, you don't casually drop shit like that when people have food in their mouth."

"Sorry, we were talking about money, and I thought I should let you know. I don't want you to think I would keep things from you. Plus, it's even more since I invested. And—"

"Stop." Brax put his hand up and cut me off. "First, I'm happy you have money, a lot of money, but, baby, that's yours. We won't need to touch any of that to live. Might need to dip into it to send our kids to college, though."

"Kids? As in plural?" I asked as I stopped the fork right at my lips.

"Well, yeah, I would like to have at least three or four."

Are you crazy? Is what I wanted to ask, but Brax's face dropped, and I knew where his thoughts went.

"How come you and Stormy didn't have more kids?" It took him a minute, and it left me wondering if he would even answer.

"She had a hard time carrying BJ. At delivery, they ended up having to give her an emergency C-section because he was too big for her to push out." He took a deep breath and glanced down at my stomach before he brought his eyes back to mine. "After they delivered him, she started bleeding above what was normal. They ended up having to take one of her ovaries because of a small tumor that had ruptured. The way it was wrapped around the ovary, the doctors were even surprised she got pregnant to begin with."

"Sweetie, I'm sorry," I said and rubbed his forearm.

"She didn't take any birth control after, but she never got pregnant again."

My heart was breaking for him, and there wasn't anything I wouldn't do for Brax to put the light back in his eyes.

"I imagine you as an awesome dad to BJ, and I have no doubt you will be just as awesome with our child. So, sweetie, you want four kids—I'm game. We can go to the crazy house together."

"Goddamn, I love you." I was snatched off the stool and in Brax's arms being kissed before I knew what had happened. After he kissed me dizzily, he sat me back down on the stool and then went and pulled a box out of the fridge. "Want to celebrate?"

"If that's the famous cheesecake, you bet your ass." Brax laughed and set the box on the island and lifted the lid.

"Don't be stingy. I want a sizeable piece. I am eating for two."

"How about we share?" Brax chuckled, slid the box to me, and handed me a clean fork.

I took the first bite, then moaned around the fork. When I went for the second bite, I looked up at Brax. "My ass is going to be so wide." Brax winked.

"And I will love every inch." It was my turn to laugh.

"Hmm," I said and closed my eyes, leaned on the back of the bar stool, and ran my hand across my stomach. "Ah, I'm so full. I don't think I can force another bite."

"Come on, we'll go work it off," Brax said, and lifted me into his arms.

"Do we have a bed? I haven't even been upstairs."

"Yeah, nice and big. The only thing I bought new after I got here. I'm not exactly a small man."

"And aren't I lucky."

"In about two minutes, both of us are going to be," Brax said, and kicked the door shut. and was true to his words.

Chapter Fourteen

Ghost

"Didn't expect you'd be eager to get down to business this morning," Flirt remarked as we walked around the empty building where the club's gym would be.

"Shit, I imagine it had to do with visitors at his place," Crusher piped in and slapped me on the back. "Carly, Sami, and Bailey hit his place this morning. I tried to hold Carly off, but was informed they needed to go early because they wanted to help Luna get settled in."

"I'd go with just wanting to be nosey," Speed mumbled.

"Brother, are you not the president of this club?" Jag asked and looked at Crusher. I chuckled when Crusher flipped him off.

"Hey, once shower sex was offered, I kind of lost that caring feeling about the brother's Saturday morning getting interrupted. Am I proud of that? No. But I am relaxed."

"Wow, you have such a big heart," Jag sneered.

"First, I know I have a heart because it was pounding in my chest when Carly's lips wrapped—"

"Enough!" Speed yelled, cutting Crusher off, and catching the rest of us off guard. "Can we act like we have dicks instead of vaginas? I get enough of that at home. And you," he pointed at Crusher, "may be our prez, but I don't want visuals of what my sister does with you. Jag, you're my brother, but you need to pull the stick out of your ass and stop snapping before one of us tires of your grouchy ass and snaps on you instead."

I turned and dropped the end of the measuring tape on the floor. I walked backward while the tape rolled out, to hide the twitching of my lips. That had to be the most Speed said at one time, and the interaction between these men was always amusing. Though I was close to them all, there was nothing that compared to the bond they shared with each other from growing up together. It would be hard to miss even if a person didn't know their background.

"His problem isn't a stick, it's blue balls or should I say frozen balls," Coast said as he walked over and placed his foot on the end of the tape to hold it in place.

"Look who's talking. Oh wait, you're not because she'd have to stop avoiding you, so you could talk to her," Jag shot back.

I looked over at Flirt, and he grinned and shrugged. Wouldn't be the first time we had to break up a fight.

"Alright, knock the crap off. Damn, you guys have been some testy assholes lately. I was trying to give Ghost a hard time, and you bunch could ruin a wet dream," Crusher said just as the door swung open and Ally and Neely ran in with Devil behind them.

"I don't have wet dreams. Right, Daddy?" Ally said as she stopped in front of Speed. "Momma says big girls don't wet their panties."

Speed looked at Crusher and lifted a brow, then squatted down to Ally. I chalked the floor, then started rolling the measuring tape up and worked not to laugh while I said a silent prayer that Luna and I had a boy.

"You sure are a big girl. Uncle Russ was just telling us about when he was little and wet himself when he was sleeping," Speed said, then stood.

"Gross," Neely said and wrinkled her nose while she looked at Crusher. There was a brief pause, then we all laughed at Crusher's expense while he glared at us.

I wasn't sure who the adults were in the room, the little girls or us. What I was sure of—Ally and Neely were Karma's payback for my brothers.

"If you as..." Crusher cleared his throat, "If we're done goofing off, can we get back to business?"

"Please, I just got here. Goofing off is far from what I've been doing," Dev said.

"What have you been doing, brother? When we were ready to leave, you said you would be right behind us because you overslept," Coast asked.

"I would have been here sooner, but Bailey ran out with the other women to your house," Devil said and pointed at me, "leaving Neely with me. Do you know how long it takes to get a pint-sized person to eat and brush their teeth? That's not adding in that she changed outfits twice. I mean really, she's three. How early do females pick up that trait? Then her hair. Do I look like someone who knows how to braid? It takes forever just to do a ponytail."

"Well, at least that explains the mixed matched clothes," Flirt said low enough to Coast and me, so no one else heard.

"How'd you end up with Ally because she was with Sami?" Speed asked.

"They were helping Luna unpack, and Ally was bored. Bailey called and caught us going out the door and asked if I would pick up Ally because they called Sue and she agreed to watch the girls. So... there you go," Devil said and held his hands palm up. "Ally wanted to stop and see you before I dropped them at Sue's."

"We need to work on the bikes. We lost time, and the buyers are anxious to get them. Don't want to have a delay," Speed said.

"We won't be much longer here. And with the women occupied, we can work on them this afternoon. What is your opinion on splitting the space, Ghost?" Crusher asked.

"Since the club is going to purchase the building, I think we should definitely have the space divided, and each side should have its own entrance. The door there now would be on the gym side. If we place the wall where I just marked with chalk, the door for the massage side would then be centered for its space and blend in as if it had always been there. Better chance to get more clientele if it has its own entrance. Not a lot of folks are gonna want to walk into the gym area to get to the massage side. Especially if they aren't members of the gym. The wall could run here," I walked to the front wall, "to the back, to include splitting the storage room between both."

"Going to need an office area. That will shrink the storage space even more," Coast said and walked to the doorway that led to the storage area in the back.

"An office on each side of the new wall should be doable. A door could be put in, which would allow us to go between to each business through the offices without having to leave the building," I said and pointed to where the door could go if we agreed with the plan.

"Shit, Ghost, you really thought this out. Hell, instead of running this for the club, start your own construction company," Flirt said. "You've done repairs at almost every business the club owns. Why don't you do the renovations on this place?"

"Brother, thanks for the vote of confidence. Not sure I know enough about building to take that on," I said, and smacked his shoulder.

"Ghost, if it is something you would be interested in, the club would back you. Lots of guys in the club have construction experience. Dare worked for a big construction company until he threw his back out," Crusher said.

"You should talk to him, brother. Hell, he'd probably want in and would work, too, as long as he didn't have to do the heavy lifting," Jag added.

"Appreciate it. It's something to think about it."

"You could test your skills with this place," Flirt said and turned to me.

"Not if the club wants this place opening soon and making money," I chuckled. "Building the dividing wall and enclosing an area to make a room is one thing. Cutting the brick on the outside structure to add a door is above my skill level. Not to mention I need a license before I could even get the permits." I'd never thought of having my own business. And definitely never a construction company. I'd always tinkered with things growing up and helped my dad in his workshop where he made furniture as a hobby. I'd even worked for a construction business for a summer when I was sixteen. I picked up a few things if it was slow and the guys had time to teach me, which was rare. I mostly was used for cleanup or hauling materials around.

"I think that is a great idea, but it also creates a problem. Who's going to oversee these two businesses?" Coast asked, and it reminded me of Luna.

"Talking of jobs, Luna asked if any of the club businesses might need help," I said and looked at Crusher.

"I'm shocked, brother. You just got her here, and she is trying to escape already." Flirt chuckled when I flipped him off.

"She could probably have her pick of where. I know the garage could use a receptionist because those fuc... I mean, those suckers have the worst phone skills. Surprised they get any repeat business," Crusher said.

"They get the repeat business because they're beyond good at their jobs. But Payton shouldn't be allowed to be near the phone. Last time I was in there, he told some woman who called to see what it was going to cost for some repair to her engine. He listened, told her approximately how much the repair was going to cost her, and she must have been shocked. Anyway, Payton tells her he bet she didn't question the price when she had her nails done or the cost of some product to make her look younger. Crap, Roscoe wouldn't even say that to a woman. And we all know how he is," Coast said and laughed.

"Sami isn't going to go back to Soft Tails, so Tank could probably use some help. He likes the day-to-day managing but says dealing with the women is driving him insane," Speed said, then leaned through the doorway to check on Ally and Neely when he heard them laughing.

"Ghost, just ask where she'd like to work. Brothers will make a place for her."

"Thanks, Prez. I'll let her know."

"If you decide on the construction business, we could put two people to oversee these places. One for the gym side and one for the massage side," Devil brought up.

"Not sure she's interested in full-time. I'm hoping after the baby comes, she'll want to stay home." I wanted her to stay home because I wasn't too keen on the working idea. But mostly, it had to do with wanting her close.

"Yeah, I can see you now with the baby strapped to your back while you're swinging a hammer or helping someone with one of the machines." I looked at Flirt and all he did was smirk.

"Brother, I hope the woman who finally snags you is a hardass," I said, and the others agreed.

"Won't happen," Flirt replied, and I shook my head. Poor bastard thought he had a choice. There was no choice when the right woman presented herself.

"We'll let you be delusional and just have fun at your expense when it happens. Kind of like you did with us," Devil said, then laughed when Flirt narrowed his eyes at him.

"Alright, if we can't talk Ghost into doing the construction on this place, let's use the guys who built onto the garage for us," Crusher suggested.

"They did an excellent job, and they got it done fast," Jag responded.

"Cost wasn't bad either," Coast added.

"I'll call them, see when they can come by and look at the place to give us an estimate," Devil said and pulled out his phone.

We moved back into the main part and watched Ally and Neely run around space while we waited for Devil to complete his call.

"Mick said he'd be available to swing by in about two hours if we wanted him to do it today," Devil said to us as he held his hand over the phone.

"We could grab something at the diner if everyone wants to wait," I suggested.

"Sounds good to me. Might as well get that part over with," Crusher said.

"Do me and Neely get to go?" Ally asked and smiled at Speed. He nodded, and she and Neely jumped up and down.

"No way you can be hungry, squirt. I just fed you at the house," Devil said as he disconnected the call, then bent in front of Neely. She stopped jumping, and the smile left her face.

Christ, Luna had to have a boy. If I had a daughter and she gave me that look of disappointment, I'd give her anything to clear it away.

"You're going with us to the diner, Neely. I just don't know where you're gonna put any more food," Devil said, palmed her face and stood.

"Hey," Neely said as she looked up at Devil, who smiled down at her.

"Ha, got away before you could do it back," he chuckled, and his smile spread.

"There's always room for pancakes," Ally said.

Speed smiled, bent, and grabbed Ally around the waist and swung onto his shoulders. "Got that right, spider monkey."

"Well, let's lock up and head to Thelma's place. I could use more coffee," Jag said, and headed for the door.

The rest of us followed, and once outside, Jag locked the door. Within ten minutes, we were at the diner and ordering food. I ate and listened to the conversation, but my mind kept rolling over the idea of a construction company.

Chapter Fifteen

Luna

"I'm so glad you girls came by. Well, maybe not at eight thirty in the morning, but looking around now, I can't complain." I leaned against the counter with Bailey while Carly and Sami sat on the other side of the island on the stools.

I hadn't known what to think when they showed up and was a little uncomfortable after Ghost first left and I was alone with them. But Sami, Bailey, and Carly made it easy. They talked to me as if I'd always been a part of their group.

"I told this one," Sami used her thumb to point at Carly, "that we should wait, but she doesn't listen."

"I listen. I just chose not to follow what you say," Carly said, and stuck her tongue out at Sami.

"I can't wait for her to have a kid," Sami said to me and Bailey, then swiftly turned her head to Carly. "I'm sorry. I swear I'm losing a brain cell a day with this one."

"Sami, it is fine. I'm not going to break down every time someone mentions kids or when I see a pregnant woman. I'm okay. Mac said there is no reason I shouldn't get pregnant naturally. It will happen. She said after the stress on my body from getting shot, and my worry of being cleared to go back to work could be a factor. Not every woman gets pregnant at the drop of a hat." Carly picked up her glass and took a drink. "And it is going to piss me off if everyone walks on eggshells around me," she added and looked at Bailey as she sat the glass back down.

"Oh my God, we haven't told a soul. How do you even know?" Bailey asked, and Carly smiled.

"I'm not a deputy just because I look good in the uniform," Carly said, and continued to drink her tea. Sami chuckled and got off the stool to hug Bailey, then she sat back down and looked at Carly.

"I can't believe you knew and didn't say anything. It's so unlike you." Sami laughed when Carly rolled her eyes.

"I didn't want to ruin their news. I don't blab everything. And if Lance hasn't told the others, it will be a first. They gossip more than women."

"Only amongst themselves, because if Kane knows, he hasn't said one word," Sami said and looked at me and raised a brow.

I held my hands up. "Nope, if Brax knows, he's not shared either. And considering the men filled me about you girls except for Lance, I lean toward he hasn't told his brothers."

"I'm still waiting for Carly to tell us how she found out," Bailey said, and eyed Carly.

"Geez, I pay attention. It's part of being a cop, that's all. Before the guys left for San Diego, you and Lance were standing on the porch. He kissed the breath out of you, then he ran his hand gently over your stomach and that damn smirk was on his face." Carly grabbed the pitcher from the island and filled her glass.

"I get why she wanted to wait," I said, and three sets of eyes pierced me. "It's a lot to take in and wrap your head around the fact you have a little person growing inside you. Brax and I didn't use condoms when we ran into each other, so the possibility was there. But you're still not prepared. I missed my period and thought I was just being paranoid and asking for problems. Until morning sickness struck. Hard to rationalize it away when your face is over the toilet bowl or you're staring into a trash can."

"Been there, twice," Sami said, and rubbed her baby bump. "Only been like a week since it stopped for me. Crazy how you hit that second trimester and bam, it's gone."

"Ugh, I've got almost two months more of it," I moaned, and Sami smiled.

"It will go by quick. And, Bailey, I didn't know you and Devil were trying," Sami said, and Bailey chuckled.

"Because we weren't. I missed three straight days of my birth control with everything going on. Getting back with Lance, moving in with him, and then Neely coming to live with us. I was a little worried about continuing to take them since I missed more than one day, so I spoke with Mac." Bailey chuckled, then continued. "Mac said chances were slim, but we'd do a quick blood test to make sure. That way, since I already missed a few, I could start back after my cycle and get back on track. It meant Lance would have to wear condoms for a month, no big deal there. So, we did the blood test and here I am—in a new job, raising a three-year-old, and pregnant."

"Now that Carly ruined your surprise, are you going to tell your mom and Lance's dad?" Sami asked, and Carly rolled her eyes.

"I guess we should, because I don't want to catch hell if my mom finds out before I get a chance. And to be honest, it has killed Lance not to tell anyone and everyone. He's quite proud of knocking me up. Something about the precision of a military man and hitting the target with such a small window."

"God, I can't imagine how I'm going to do it with one. Scares the hell out of me. And both of you are going to have two children to deal with," I said, amazed how Sami and Bailey were so calm.

"I'll admit at first when Lance brought Neely home, I figured I would be the one having to do everything for her. And don't get me wrong, I would have. I love Neely. I know she probably saw things a small child should never see, and then add in a brother, a new home, even though it was best for her, it was a change from what she knew. A big change. But Lance dove right in, which I think helped improve her transition because she only had a couple of nightmares, and he would stay with her until she fell back to sleep. Her shyness had more to do with being told to be quiet and stay out of the way. He's been good for her, and he's pulled her out of the shyness. He loves her, which I think shocked him. It came so quickly. She knows it, feels it, and returns it. After everything he told me about when he found her, it's probably her first experience with anyone caring for her. They've bonded as only siblings can. And they are amusing to watch together."

"Damn hormones," I said and wiped at the tears that escaped the corners of my eyes.

"I know. I cry at commercials. It's annoying," Sami sniffed.

"He's going to make a great dad, Bailey," Carly said, and laid a hand on top of Bailey's.

"I think so, too," Bailey agreed.

"Well, I'm kind of thinking the guys need to wrap it up twice," Carly said, and chuckled when Sami slapped her arm. "I wasn't talking about your men. Kind of late for that anyway, don't you think? I'm talking Dom, Max, and Emery."

"Dom's hot for some ice princess from what I could make out from the guys teasing him when we were traveling here," I said, and Sami grinned.

"I don't know about hot as he wants to jump her. It's more like she gets under his skin and his temper gets hot," Sami said, and then explained how Dom had met River.

"Yeah, and what is the saying about when ya bitch too much?" I said, and Carly pointed at me.

"Exactly! All you have to do is mention her and he goes from calm to explosive in one minute flat. And don't get me started on Emery and Mac. He goes at her, and she dodges better than a boxer. That man has it bad. How Mac is holding her own is beyond me because the man fills out a pair of jeans," Carly said and fanned herself.

"Does Russ know you have a crush on Emery?" Sami asked.

"It's not a crush, it is admiration for a man who wears his clothes well. I have the same admiration for my man and the others, too." Sami shook her head at Carly's explanation.

"So... I can tell Kane you think he looks good in his clothes?" Sami asked, and Bailey and I laughed when Carly lip curled, and she made a disgusted face.

"I know you think you're being cute, but one, the man needs no ego boost. And two, he's my brother, we share the same genes. It would be like saying I was ugly. Though opposites in looks, mine are better."

"Not just genes you share," Sami said under her breath as she moved to stand between Bailey and me.

"Was that supposed to be an insult?" Carly asked and rolled her eyes.

"Can you be insulted?" Bailey asked, and Carly looked at her, then chuckled.

"No, not really," Carly said, and we laughed at her honesty.

"When I talked with Max, he didn't strike me as the type to hold off on what he wants when it comes to women. Or did I read him wrong?" I asked, hoping for a little more insight into Brax's best friend.

"Nope, you nailed him. Max won't wait. But I bet it takes him a bit when he comes across the right woman to realize she's it for him," Bailey said.

"When I worked at Soft Tails, I thought for sure he was into Syn the way he watched her, but then nothing." Sami stood and walked her glass to the sink.

"Oh, he was into Syn. It just didn't last. He doesn't want a woman to be his slave. The woman is going to need to be strong, but able to hand over control to him for sex. Syn isn't exactly what he's looking for," Carly said, and handed her glass to Sami when she reached for it.

"Look at you, Ms. Intuitive," Bailey said.

"Whatever, bite me," Carly replied and stood. "Now that we've gotten to know Luna, helped her unpack, and had a good gossip session, let's go outside and look at her bike. I've been dying to see it up close. Plus, I'm stoked that you ride. I can't get these bitches interested," Carly said and headed out of the kitchen.

I took mine and Bailey's glasses to the sink before I followed the women. As I walked through the house, I looked around the living room. With their help, Brax and I were well on our way to settling into the place. We still needed some things, but it was at least a start.

"Where is the best place to buy furniture?" I asked as Carly opened the front door and we all walked out.

Before we reached my bike, we had a plan set for the upcoming week. And as Carly and I talked about the best roads to ride, any nerves about moving and settling into a new place were washed away.

I was home.

Chapter Sixteen

Ghost

As I rode up, Luna sat on the porch with her feet crossed on the rail, looking more than relaxed. I pulled to the side, shut off my bike, dismounted, and made my way to the porch.

"Did you have a good day, baby?" I asked as I walked up the few steps.

"I did. How about you? Is the building going to suit the club's need?"

"Yeah, everything looks doable. Already met with the contractor, he'll work up an estimate. Long as it doesn't come in outlandishly high, the club will have two more businesses."

"That's great. You want to sit out here with me for a bit, or do you want to go in?"

"Let me grab a beer and I'll be back."

I went inside, grabbed a beer out of the fridge and poured Luna a glass of tea. As I headed back through the house, I glanced around the living room and noticed the boxes were gone and the books were on the shelf along with my Blue-rays. My military plaques and the few pictures I had were leaning against the wall. But what caught my attention was the wooden boxes that sat on the mantle of the fireplace with pictures of various sizes spread out beside them.

Sitting the drinks down on the end table, I moved to the fireplace and picked up the first photo. BJ's gray eyes, so like mine, looked out from it. He was four when it was taken, and he wore elbow and knee pads with his biking helmet on while he straddled the seat on his first big boy bike. I sat it down and moved to the next one. He stood on the top step of the bus, the first day he'd ridden it to school, a smile on his face and his hand waving goodbye. There were various pictures of Stormy with BJ, too. But the picture that captured my attention was the one in the middle.

I picked the photo up and with my free hand, I ran my fingers down the glass in the frame. Looking at it, the same feeling surfaced from the day it was taken.

"When the women helped me unpack today, I came across a box with the pictures and a few photo albums in it."

I hadn't heard Luna come in. I kept my back to her and continued to hold the picture.

"Yeah, I never unpacked them. They were part of the things I had shipped here. I never could bring myself to pull them out."

"Are you upset I did?" I heard the unsureness in her voice when she asked.

"I'd missed BJ's birth. This picture was taken a few hours after I got back from my first mission as a SEAL. It was the first time I saw and held him. He was three weeks old. I've never felt anything close to what I felt in that moment."

I set the picture back in its place, then waved my hand to include them all when I spoke again.

"Out of these. I was gone when seventy-five percent of them were taken." I laid a hand on top of each box. "They were mine to protect, and I failed them. These are reminders of my failure."

"Bullshit!" Luna said as her arms wrapped around my waist, and she laid her head against my back. "You can't control everything. They didn't die because you weren't there to protect them. They died because some asshole spent the night getting sloshed and didn't care about his own life enough to not drive. Stormy and BJ were the casualty of his disregard. Look at me."

Luna loosened her arms enough for me to turn around, then she tightened them again and tilted her head back to look up at me.

"You're the best man I know. I didn't set any of it out to make you feel bad. They were a part of you, Brax. Everything that happens, every fraction of our lives, makes us who we are. And you wouldn't be the man you are without having them in your life. Regardless of the amount of time."

"When I first got here, guilt that I was alive ate at me. And now, as irrational as it is, guilt that I'm getting a second chance at happiness."

I kissed Luna's forehead, then led her to the couch. After we sat, I handed her the glass of iced tea and picked up my beer.

"That is stupid. If the situation was reversed, you wouldn't want Stormy sitting around brooding. And if every time you walk in this room throws you into the mood, we'll put the stuff back in the box and shove it in the back of a closet." Luna took a drink of her tea.

"Did you just call me stupid and a brooder?" I asked and tipped the beer bottle up and took a swig.

"If the biker boots fit," Luna said unashamedly, and placed her glass on the coffee table.

"You always could pull me out of a mood. Even when we were kids."

"Because you were stupid and brooded then, too."

I chuckled, set my bottle on the end table, grabbed Luna, and pulled her across my lap. Raising my hand, I placed it on the back of head, then ran it down her short blond hair.

"Thank you for setting them out. You didn't have to do that." I kissed the top of her head. "This is our home, and I don't want you to be uncomfortable."

"Brax, they were your family, your life before us. Stormy was my friend at one time. Would I do anything that made me uncomfortable?"

"No, baby," I said, pulled her to me until she leaned against me and laid her head on my shoulder. I moved my hand to her back and rubbed it.

"And I wouldn't do anything to hurt you. But, Brax, you can't hide from the past, and you don't want to forget the things from it you loved. I don't want you to ever feel you have to hide your feelings from me." Luna placed her hand over my heart and turned her head and kissed the underside of my chin before settling back in.

I rested my cheek on the top of her head and closed my eyes. When I opened them, the light was fading from the room.

"Did we fall asleep?" Luna stretched in my arms.

"Looks that way. You hungry, baby?" I asked when I heard her stomach growl.

"Maybe a little. Come into the kitchen and let's see what we can throw together. Thank God, they stocked some basics, but we are going to have to go to the grocery sooner rather than later." Luna got off my lap, and we headed to the kitchen.

"We can go tomorrow if you're up to it. I'll show you around town, take you around to the club businesses, so you'll know which ones are ours." I opened the fridge and pulled out the pack of steaks and set them on the counter. "How about I throw those on the grill?"

"Okay, and I'll throw a salad together."

"Salad?" I wrinkled my nose, and Luna laughed.

"Such a guy. Salad is good for you. One cannot live on meat alone. Besides, I saw potato salad in one of the bowls."

"Well, good, because lettuce and shit should be left to the rabbits. I gotta have meat and potatoes to survive."

"Can't have you whittling down to nothing," Luna said and shook her head. I smacked her ass as she walked around me.

I found a pan and tongs, then unpackaged the steaks and located some seasonings. Luna pulled out the salad makings and a cutting board and knife. We moved around each other in the kitchen like we'd done it forever.

When I brought the steaks in, Luna had the table set and the sides set out and ready. While we ate, she told me about her time with the women, and that they set up a time to go shopping next week. She smiled as she talked, which made me smile. I wanted her to be happy here and accept this as her home. A home with me.

"You don't mind if I look for new living room furniture and some other stuff for the house?"

"Baby, you can change anything you want. The only furniture I bought new was the bedroom. I'll give you my credit card and you buy whatever you think we need." I leaned in and kissed her, then stood and carried our plates to the sink.

"That reminds me. I'm going to need to change banks, switch my insurance and tag for my bike. First, I'm going to need to transfer my driver's license. Maybe we can hit the driver's license place Monday or sometime next week?"

"Both the licensing offices are in the courthouse. We can swing by next week to do it or another day. You got thirty days to transfer them. As for the bank, I can take you to the one I use. But you don't have to worry about that right now." I wrapped her in my arms after she put the leftover potato salad in the fridge.

"I've got money, Brax, and I will not let you spend all of yours while I sit on mine. Don't argue. I'm here because I let you strong arm me. I won't always be so tranquil."

"With me, you will be. Because you can't tell me no." I bent and swooped her up in my arms and started toward the stairs.

"You don't have to be such a smug bastard," Luna said and wrapped her arms around my neck. "Maybe I just like using your body."

"Well, use away, baby. Don't let me stop you," I said and laughed when she smacked my shoulder.

I walked through the doorway of the bedroom and kicked the door shut. After I stripped her naked and removed my clothes, I let her use my body until we both were exhausted, and our eyes were heavily lidded.

Chapter Seventeen

Luna

It had been an enjoyable week. Even my morning sickness hadn't seemed too awful. Brax and I had spent time together getting reacquainted. Being with him every day and night, it was easy to forget we'd had years apart. We went into town, and he showed me the businesses, introduced me to his brothers. We had lunch at the diner where I met Tank and Bull's mother, Thelma. I transferred my driver's license and tagged my bike. I was now a legal resident of the great state of Washington.

The women and I had spent an entire day together and literally shopped till we dropped. Somehow, we squeezed in a visit to Bailey's work. She introduced me to

Dr. Monroe and my first appointment was scheduled. The day had been productive. I purchased new furniture for the living room. A bedroom set for one of the spare rooms. A desk for the small room off the kitchen. The only room empty was the one closest to our room. We would fix it for the baby when it was time. The kitchen even had a new table. One that would seat six. After towels, linen, and rugs, we hit a couple of clothing stores and the Harley shop. Warm weather wear was a necessity I hadn't thought about until my first morning when I stepped outside on the back deck with my juice. I was going to miss coffee, but when Brax found out I had still been drinking it, it wasn't worth the fight.

"Baby, I know that look. The room is fine as it is." Brax wrapped his arms around me and rested his chin on the top of my head.

"You're only saying that because you don't want to move the furniture around again."

"As it is, I'm not sure any of the brothers will drop by again." Brax chuckled and released me. "You ready to go? I want to check in with Mick, see how far they've gotten, then catch Dare at Soft Tails."

"Please, like they would pass on unlimited beer and food because a little work might be involved."

"True." Brax chuckled. "But no matter, the couch has been on every wall, and it looks best where it is. You even said so yourself as we moved it to that spot—twice."

"Aww, you're so funny," I said and turned my head and gave him a quick peck. "I'm ready. So, after the gym, we are swinging by Soft Tails?"

"Yeah, but didn't we discuss you weren't working there?"

"Don't get your panties in a wad. Tank asked me if I would look over the list of headliners he put together. That was a great idea he had about bringing a new one in each month for a variety and to boost business. He wants to see if I recognize any of the names and if I know anything about them." I sat and pulled my boots on, then stood. "Are you going to have a problem if I help at the garage three days a week? They can really use the help, Brax. Their filing system sucks and while we were there, the phone rang twenty-five times in an hour."

"Not happy about you working at all."

I sighed. We'd been round and round about me going to work. But I knew if I didn't have something to fill a little time, I would go nuts.

"If you would start up your own company, I could handle your books and paperwork." I grabbed my jacket, and he took it from me and held it open for me while I slipped my arms in.

"You really think I could run a construction company?"

"Sweetie, you can do anything you set your mind to. You said there are a lot of guys in the club that have experience. And you can always hire outside the club to find skills none of you have. Even Flirt and the others thought it was a good idea."

"I've got two businesses to get up and running for the club."

"Once those are ready to open, there won't be anything to do but oversee the everyday operation of them. And can you honestly tell me that sitting in an office each day is your dream job?"

"Working with my hands every day has its appeal. That's why I wanted to stop at Soft Tails. Dare should be there, and I was hoping to chat with him about it. Now let's get going. We can go out the back. I rolled the bikes out of the garage. Might need to build onto the garage this spring. Tight fit with my truck and the bikes in there."

"Probably because the truck is a monster." We headed out the back door and walked across the yard to the detached garage. My bike was beside Brax's. As I reached them, I looked at his and then at mine.

"What's wrong, baby?" Brax asked as he straddled his bike.

"Well, I like your Black Hawk symbol on the gas tank. Did you get that done somewhere in town?"

"Coast painted it for me. All our bikes have it. We can get yours done. Carly has it on hers. I honestly hadn't thought about it. You've not been to Speed and Sami's yet. The garage they build the custom bikes in is behind their place. I'll check with Coast, see when he can get to it. They're busy with an order right now, though."

I got on my bike and ran my hand over the Ops' and Lady Riders' symbols. It would be sad to see them gone, but like the old saying, *'Out with the old and in with the new.'*

"Thanks, sweetie." Brax nodded, then we put our helmets on and we cranked the bikes. It was my first time riding my bike since I moved there. The vibration and the rumble of the pipes as we pulled out were familiar and comforting. As we reached the gate, the prospect on duty had it open, and we hadn't even had to slow. At the end of the drive, we turned right toward town, and I opened the bike up. Nothing compared to the wind and open road in front of you.

The ride felt great and ended all too quickly as we hit the outskirts of town. We slowed as we rode on the main road until we reached the building and pulled to the curb and parked. I killed the engine and pulled my helmet off while Brax did the same.

"Looks as if they're working in the back. Shouldn't be in there too long, then we'll go by Soft Tails. Being as Monday they're closed, but Tank, Dare, and a few of the others should be there, its delivery day for the bar and kitchen."

"Sounds good," I said as I dismounted and stepped onto the sidewalk.

After Brax talked with Mick, the contractor, and we looked over what they had done so far, which was splitting the storage area up and building the wall between the two, we were back on our bikes and headed to the strip club in under an hour.

The parking lot at Soft Tails had several bikes lined in the front of the building when we pulled in. Once we were off the bikes and walking through the door was when we heard raised voices coming from the kitchen area, which was behind the bar. Stem looked over his shoulder from his spot at the bar, where he emptied a box and lined the bottles of liquor on the shelves.

"Enter there at your own risk," Stem said and thumbed toward the kitchen.

"What is Perry bitchin' about?" Ghost asked.

"Does the man need a reason?" Tank came through the swinging door just as Stem spoke.

"Hey, brother. Luna," Tank said and ran his hand down his face. "Jesus, I didn't know how much Sami kept his ass in line."

"What set him off this time?" Brax asked.

"Hell, the liquor delivery came, and Dare was checking off as Lock stacked the boxes inside the door until they were done unloading. The extra inventory would go into the storage room after the bar was stocked. Perry yelled at him because the food delivery pulled up and the boxes were in the way. Then Prez sent Cobalt to help after he was done with his shift at the gate. He pulled up in time to help with the food and Perry jumped him because he put the shit in the wrong place in the walk-in," Tank said, blew out a breath, and grinned. "I came out because I heard him yelling from the office. Shit, I thought someone broke into the kitchen."

"I'm pretty sure your mention of a change in the menu didn't help either," Dare said as he joined us.

"What the hell, Tank?" Brax asked.

"I thought it would give the old bastard something else to focus on."

Dare shook his head. "Oh, it worked. Took his focus right off Lock and Cobalt and moved to thoughts of stabbing you," Dare said, and slapped Tank on the back.

"Crazy, is what he is. Now, please tell me you are here to help me, Luna?" Tank asked.

"If it's going over the list of strippers, then yes. To help with the kitchen tyrant, no," I said, and Dare laughed.

"Damn, she catches on quick, Ghost," Dare said, and Brax slung his arm over my shoulders.

"Brains and beauty," Brax said, leaned over and kissed the top of my head. "And mine."

"Like that isn't obvious," Tank said and chuckled. "It won't take long to go over the list. It's back in the office if you can look at it now."

"Yeah, that would be good," I answered.

"Dare, if you got a few minutes, I'd like to talk with you while Luna's with Tank," Brax said, and Dare nodded.

"We can sit at one of the tables. What's up?" Dare asked.

"Got a proposition for you," Brax said, and just like that, the two men moved away and sat at a table.

"Well, guess that leaves us," Tank said, and motioned for me to follow him.

In Tank's office, I sat in the chair in front of the desk. He had a nice list of some of the top strippers who bought in good crowds wherever they were showcased.

"So, what do you think?" he asked.

"Good list." I reached for a pen off the desk and marked through two names. "Gonna want to stay away from the couple I marked off. Rumor is they don't bring a take like they used to do, and their attitudes aren't worth any rise in revenue."

"What about the rest?"

"Few names on here I've not heard of, but they could be up and comers. If their guaranteed amount isn't much, you could try them. You're going to want to stick to weekends only for the spotlight spots. One every two months to start, so it will give you an idea if it's going to be worth the club's time. You draw in a client base, then move to a showcase for a month. Line them up and have them booked, then advertise beforehand," I said and continued down the list, rating the ones I knew with stars.

"I really appreciate you taking the time to look at this. Gonna be a problem if I ask for help if I come up against something I don't know how to do or deal with?"

"Not a problem. Just call me. I'll help if I can." I handed the list back. "Number seven, Limber Lacey? Never seen her on the stage but, heard she can do shit on a pole that will bring the first night crowd back the next night." I laughed when Tank picked up a highlighter and marked the name.

We discussed a few more of the women on the list, and Tank asked a couple more questions. After we finished, I stood and so did he.

"Guess if I'm gonna pretend to run this place, I better check on Perry. He could have the prospects hung up and skinning them." I laughed at Tank as we walked out of the office and headed back into the main area.

When we turned toward the table area, I heard a woman's laughter and then saw her as she leaned her hip on the table Dare and Brax sat at. I also noticed my man had an irritated look on his face as she spoke, then ran her hand down his arm, leaning as she did to where her tank gaped open enough the men could see down the top to her breasts.

She was poured into a denim skirt that looked as if it would fit Speed's daughter. Her hair was pulled into a messy ponytail held with a clip and on her feet were flip-flops. I noticed she had a little sweat beaded on her forehead, too.

Skank was my thought as we approached the table.

"Lindy, what are you doing here?" Tank asked as we reached the table.

"Oh, sugar, I left a few things in my locker that I needed. Knew someone would be here to let me in," she said and stood from her position, then looked me over.

"You usually are at the diner on Mondays. Did you leave Ma shorthanded today?" Tank's tone of voice on the question had me glancing at him. I got the feeling it wasn't the first time Lindy had done it.

Instead of answering Tank's question, she asked him one, "Interviewing a new girl?" Then she turned and looked at Brax without waiting for Tank's answer. "Let me know when you're ready to get back in the game, big guy. Standing offer to help you get over your troubles."

Brax opened his mouth, but I didn't give him a chance to get any words out. "Ah, sugar," I used the same tone as Lindy did when she spoke to Tank. "Big guy doesn't need what you are offering. I already fucked his troubles away."

Dare turned his head away and coughed, and Brax sat there with his eyes crinkled at the edges while his lips twitched.

"Lindy, if you'd given me a chance to answer, you might not have embarrassed yourself. I would have introduced Ghost's ol' lady," Tank said, and when Lindy just stood there, he continued. "Didn't you need something out of your locker?"

"Yeah, I should grab it, so the rest of my day off isn't wasted." Lindy gave me one last look and turned to walk away.

I noticed she had a slight limp as she moved. I frowned as I watched her until she was out of sight.

"Something wrong, baby?" Brax asked, and I looked back at him.

"Black Hawk okay with their girls using?" I asked, and all three men frowned at me.

"Fuck no, had a problem a few years back with drugs running through the club, but that was cleared up. That is when Sami started managing the place," Tank answered, but still frowned at me.

"Luna, what would make you ask that?" Brax asked.

"Well, I would bet money that Lindy is using. She had several signs. Sweating while the room has a chill to it. Her hands shook a little. I'd say she is coming down and left her stash in her locker."

"Tank, you better call Crusher," Dare said, and Tank nodded and pulled his phone out.

"Damn, Luna, I didn't even notice that shit when she was standing right in front of me," Brax said, and I couldn't stop myself from at least giving him some attitude.

"Probably because you had a set of big breasts in front of your face," I said with no trace of humor.

"Bullshit, and for the record, I wouldn't have touched that even if I was told it was lined with gold and it granted wishes when you entered," Brax said. I could not hold my stern look with his expression of disgust.

"Sweetie, I always knew you had good taste," I said and moved to give him a kiss.

"Prez and VP are on their way with Speed. This is going to get ugly. Unless she has some shit on her or in that locker of hers, she'll bitch and deny it. We've not been diligent with drug testing other than when a new girl is hired. Shit, that isn't going to go over well either," Tank said.

"Hard for strippers to hide shooting up, which I'd say she is. Needle marks would be visible. There is only so much you can cover with make-up. So, I would look between her toes."

"Come on, Luna, I heard that shit hurts like a bitch. And you have to be spot on with the needle," Brax said.

"When she walked in, she had a limp and Ghost and I asked about it. She said she twisted her foot last night dancing," Dare said.

"Uh huh, yet no bruising on her ankle on foot. Bet there is some between those toes of hers. And she's been in the back a while already. Not thinking you are going to have a problem finding anything."

"Well, we are going to find out soon enough," Tank said and looked toward the door. I glanced over as Crusher, Jag, and Speed walked in.

"Showtime," Dare said and stood with Tank.

"Stay here," Brax said, and stood with other men.

Tank nodded his head toward the back when Crusher looked at him. The president nor the others had a happy face as they headed to the back with Brax, Dare, and Tank following behind.

I almost felt sorry for the woman.

Almost.

Chapter Eighteen

Ghost

"Are you sure you don't want me to go with you to the appointment?" I asked as I walked into the bedroom as Luna's head popped through the neck of the shirt she pulled on.

"I really appreciate the offer and am happy you want to be involved in everything, but... It is only the first visit of many. Bailey is working today, and I'm nervous enough without having you hover," Luna said, and pulled her jeans up. "Dammit, my pants should not be getting tight already." I watched as she worked to snap her jeans.

"I am a big man, baby." I grinned when she looked up and glared at me.

"Duh, like I don't know that. The kid can wait to grow *after* I've pushed her or him out. Finally," she said as the jeans fastened.

"Don't think you can control that, baby." I walked to the dresser and grabbed my keys.

"Can you at least let me fantasize that I'm going to be one of those women who looks like she's smuggling a basketball under her shirt? Not one who looks as if she's carrying the entire team."

"Where do you come up with this shit? It natural, and besides, you could use a little extra weight," I said and then turned around and found I was receiving the death glare.

"Sure, you say that now, but what are you going to say when I don't lose the extra weight after the baby? I'm left with saddlebags and not the kind that goes on a damn bike, either. Or breasts that sag because they don't go back to my original size. Or the elasticity in the skin at my stomach that's shot to hell, and my pussy is so loo—" I cut off Luna's tirade by wrapping my arms around her and taking her mouth with mine.

"Love ya, baby. You'll always look beautiful to me," I said when I broke the kiss. "And I won't complain one bit about walking behind you and holding up your breasts."

Luna smacked my arm. "You're such an asshole," she said, then laughed. "I better go. I don't want to be late for my appointment. You sure you don't mind me driving your truck?"

"No. I'm going to shower after you leave, then take your bike over to the garage. Coast called while you were in the shower and said he had some time this morning."

"Thought they had an order to finish?" she asked as we walked downstairs.

"They do, but Coast had detailing to do on one tank and figured he could knock yours out while he was at it."

"Oh, that's cool of him," Luna said as she dug in her purse and set the key to her bike on the island. I opened the back door for her and walked her to the truck.

I took my keys out of my pocket and unlocked the door and opened it for her. When she gripped the 'oh shit' handle to help pull herself up, I put my hands on her butt and gave her a boost.

"Want me to get you a couple of pillows to sit on?"

"Aww, you are so funny," she said as she sat down in the seat. I handed her the keys, and she started the truck, then adjusted the seat to her needs.

"Call me when you get done. That way, if I'm still at the garage, I'll head to the house to meet you." I leaned in and kissed her forehead.

"Okay, that will work. Love ya, sweetie."

"Love ya, too," I said, stepped back and closed the door. I stood where I was until she'd driven out of sight.

I went back in the house and forewent the shower until I got back from the garage. It had been a while since I'd gotten a little greasy and with my brothers behind in their bike order, they could use a couple more hands.

On Luna's bike, I was glad it was only a short ride to Speed's. I wasn't sure if I could've taken a longer ride. Flirt stepped out of the garage as I rode up and shook his head.

"Brother, I don't think that bike is made for you." I flipped him off as I dismounted, and he chuckled.

"How're the bikes coming?" I asked as I walked toward him.

"They're getting there. Coast has detailing to do on a couple. We should be done on time. Definitely would be if you'd help," Flirt said, and I slapped his back.

"I was hoping you guys could use some help. Haven't worked on a bike in a long time," I said and walked in the garage behind Flirt.

"Luna's bike outside?" Coast asked as he came out of a room in the back.

"Yeah."

"I'll get to it when I finish the flames I'm painting on the tank."

"Thanks, Coast. Appreciate you squeezing it in for her."

Crusher stood and shut off the blowtorch he was using. He lifted the safety glasses before he spoke. "Please, the woman could ask the club for anything right now, and we'd give it to her. Tank's hoping to talk her into helping him out at Soft Tails. He wants to put her in charge of hiring the strippers. Not sure if it pissed him off more that firing Lindy left him short a stripper, or now Thelma's gonna be shorthanded, too. Anyway, he said she can set her own hours. Hell, he even said she could split her time between the shop and the club."

"Tough shit. Tank's gonna have to deal on his own," I answered, and Speed grinned as he picked up the handlebars for the bike he was working on.

"Yeah, I told him there was no way you'd want her working at the club. Fuck, I hated Sami working there," Speed said.

"That's because you are a controlling bastard and didn't want your woman around all the brothers," Dev said, and Speed looked over at him and glared.

"Right, and you'd be okay with Bailey working in a strip club." Speed cocked his brow, and Devil was the one who glared.

"I don't want her working at all. But I'm not gonna fight with her over it. Plus, I spoke with Dare. He's in if I want to start up a construction business. Luna said she'd work for me if I did. And the controlling bastard I am is going to do it."

Flirt laughed. "Well, hell, that's one way to get what you want."

"Whatever you need from the club, Ghost, ask. We'll work on replacing you at the gym," Prez said.

"I can finish overseeing the renovation of the building. It will take a little time getting up and running, so I might as well have something to do in the meantime," I said, and Prez agreed.

"I'll help you get the paperwork done and file for your license. Soft Tails could be your first job," Jag said from across the bay, where he worked at a table with parts spread across.

"What? Did something happen to the place?" I asked. It had only been two days since I was there.

"No, Tank has been looking at growing the business. He suggested building on to the back and moving the stage and girls in the new section. The bar seating could be expanded with a game room with darts, a couple of pool tables. Told him to work up a plan, and we'd look at it and discuss at the next meeting. If we go for it, going to need to add on, so the job would be yours. Expect to get a good price for keeping the work in the club," Crusher said.

"Please, you'll be lucky if I don't charge you extra for having to listen to Perry gripe. Hell, at first, I thought maybe something happened to the place after Luna and I left the other day," I said, and Crusher chuckled.

"Nah, the only thing that went down after Lindy was escorted out was Tank calling in the other girls. Tank was pissed that he'd been lax in the testing since he took over. He called the other girls in and questioned them, then handed them paperwork to go get tested. Told them to have it done before they came back to work. Syn, Candie, and the others swore they weren't on anything, and none bucked about going to have the testing done.

"Tank told them that there would be no discussion if the test came back positive for anything. They'd be escorted out and told not to come back, just as Lindy had been. None of the other women knew she was using, but Syn said she had noticed changes in Lindy's personality, but only in the last three months after she started seeing a new guy. Coast and Speed did some digging. The guy is a doper. Been busted a couple of times. There won't be any trouble from firing Lindy. I told her she was lucky I didn't call the sheriff in on it," Crusher said, picked up the blowtorch and moved to the next bike.

"Hey, where is the club's newest celebrity?" Flirt asked.

"First doctor's appointment," I said, then turned and watched Coast push Luna's bike through the bay door.

"Surprised you didn't tag along," Flirt said.

"She wanted to go by herself. Besides, we aren't attached at the fucking hip," I said, and Flirt shook his head and grinned.

"Fuck off. And if you want my help, tell me what you want me to work on while I'm here. Gonna meet at the house when she gets done."

Flirt laughed. "Fine. Still good with electrical?" I nodded. "Then you can wire the gauges in that one's dash." He pointed to the dark blue with silver tint bike.

The bike was sweet looking. I walked over to it and got to work. The only talking was the occasional curse word as everyone focused on their task. I didn't know how much time had passed when my cell buzzed.

Digging it out of my pocket, I read the text.

Luna: *Leaving now. Everything is good. Tell you when I get home.*

Me: *See you at the house in about twenty, baby.*

After I texted her back, I slid the phone back into my pocket and got back to the wiring. In the time it would take Luna to get to the house, I would have it done.

I set the dash in place when I was finished and walked to the sink to wash my hands before I headed home.

"Hey, heading out. Got this one done," I said and started for the door.

"Thanks for helping, Ghost," Crusher said as he pulled his ringing cell from his pocket.

"Welcome. Just yell if ya need more help," I said, and as I reached the door, my phone rang. I pulled it out of my pocket to see Roscoe on the screen.

"Yo," I said as I walked outside, then froze as he spoke. My stomach rolled, and I clutched my chest as it tightened. Four words from Roscoe and my world shattered for the second time and took me to my knees.

"There's been an accident."

Chapter Nineteen

Luna

I heard raised voices as I surfaced. Why the hell were people yelling? I opened my eyes and the bright light caused me to close them again. But not before a piercing pain shot through my head.

"Shit, that hurts," I said and lifted a hand to my head.

"You don't want to interrupt my work," a man said, and my hand was grabbed, and my arm was brought down to my side.

"Luna, do you remember what happened?" The woman's voice sounded familiar.

With my eyes still closed, I tried to think. I'd been at the house...

"Dr. Monroe? Did I pass out?"

"Take your time, it will come to you," Dr. Monroe said softly.

"There, the last stitch. You'll barely have a scar," the man spoke again, and then I heard metal ping and the snap of rubber gloves.

A scar? From what? Then it all came flooding back. Doctor's appointment, then driving back to Black Hawk. The pickup had been on my side of the road as I came around the curve. I swerved at the same time it jerked back into its lane. When it hit the side of the truck, I slid off the road and hit the hillside. The collision jerked my head to the window on the driver's side as the airbag deployed. Then darkness.

"I was in an accident. I remember coming to in the ambulance," I said.

"Yes, you came to on the ride here. The EMT talked with you briefly before you went back out. That would be the concussion you sustained from hitting your head on the window. It's also the reason the bright lights hurt. You can open your eyes now, Luna. The nurse turned the overheads out."

"Did I cut my head?" I asked and eased my eyes open. My head still hurt, but with the lights out, it was tolerable.

The male doctor stood at the foot of the bed writing in a chart while a nurse stood on one side of the bed and Dr. Monroe stood on the other.

"Not your head. Your brow was lacerated and a tad deep. Dr. Meaznan stitched it up. He was the ER doctor who examined you when they brought you in. We are waiting for a portable ultrasound to be brought down, then we will make sure the baby is doing okay," Mac said, and patted my arm.

"Since you're here with her, Dr. Monroe, I'm going to go check on one of my other patients, and I will be back." Dr. Monroe nodded, and Dr. Meaznan waved the curtain aside and stepped out.

I moved my hands to rest on my stomach. If something happened to the baby, I wouldn't be the only one destroyed.

"Is Brax in the waiting room?" I asked.

"I was told he and the others are on their way." Mac looked at her watch. "I'm sure we will hear when they arrive."

"He is going to be out of his mind," I said and closed my eyes.

"With what he has been through, he is going to want to see for himself that you are okay. Just a few bumps and bruises," Mac said.

"I forgot, you know him through the others."

"Yes, though I don't know the men as well as I do the women. I came after Carly called Bailey at the office. Bailey said she will come after she reschedules my patients. Carly is in the waiting room, pacing. She'd been at the sheriff's station when the accident was called in."

I opened my eyes. "How long have I been here?" I asked.

"Maybe an hour. I arrived right after the ambulance." Mac turned as a nurse rushed in.

"Dr. Monroe, we have a very irate man in the ER demanding to see Ms. Madison. And he's with several others," the nurse said breathlessly. It seemed Brax had arrived.

"Show him back, Deborah," Mac said, and as the nurse turned to walk out, the curtain was drawn to the side as a man pushed a machine into the area.

"Here's the ultrasound machine that was ordered. I'll come back and get it later," the man said, and Mac nodded.

Mac plugged in the machine and hit some buttons. "Well, as soon as daddy gets here, we'll take a peek and see how the baby is doing."

"Mac?"

"Don't ask for problems, Luna. This is just a precau—"

"Luna," Brax said, cutting off Mac as he stepped through the curtain and walked straight to me. "Goddammit, you scared ten years off my fucking life."

Brax ran his hand over my head, then held my chin and gently moved my head back and forth. I raised my hand and cupped his cheek, and his eyes met mine. I saw worry and fear, and it broke my heart that I was the reason for it.

"Doc, fill me in?" Brax asked, and Mac informed him of everything she knew.

"The lump she got from the window, the brow not sure. Dr. Meaznan cleaned out a couple of shards of plastic from the laceration. Figured the airbag's force broke her sunglasses and cut it that way."

"I'm going to be okay, Brax," I said.

He cleared his throat, then I watched his nostrils flare as he took a deep breath. "The baby?"

"Well, you showed up just in time. We are about to check on it," Mac said as she moved beside the bed and rolled the machine closer.

Brax moved until he stood by my head and faced the screen. I grabbed his hand as Mac lifted my gown and adjusted it after she propped my legs in the stirrups. Once she inserted the wand, she turned the machine on.

"Ready, Mom and Dad?" she asked, and neither Brax nor I spoke, we only nodded. "Alright, here we go."

"I don't know how you tell what is what," I said and squinted at the monitor.

"I'm with you there, baby," Brax said and squeezed my hand.

"Everything looks wonderful. I'd hoped since you are going into your seventh week, we'd get a decent picture. It couldn't get much better than this," Mac said and looked at us and smiled.

"Thank God," Brax said, and leaned over and kissed my forehead. "Want to tell us what we are looking at?"

"Well, first let's see if we can pick up a heartbeat." Mac messed with a couple of buttons, and the thump-thump-thump sounded.

Tears filled my eyes as I listened to the sound and focused on the screen. I couldn't believe the sound was coming from the little spot on the monitor.

"Oh my God, it looks like a raisin. I knew I was pregnant, and a tiny life grew inside me, but I don't really think the magnitude of that had sunk in until now," I said in awe.

Mac pointed out the head and the spots where the ears, nose, and mouth were. After she had done that, it was easier to see.

"Does their shadow always reflect like that?" Brax asked as he leaned in closer to the monitor. Mac grinned.

"No, that isn't a shadow. That would be baby number two," she said and looked at both of us and waited.

Brax straightened and looked at me, then back to the screen. If I hadn't been overwhelmed myself, the parlor of his skin would have had me worried.

I looked back at Mac. "Twins don't run in my family. Brax?" I asked, and he blinked a few times, then ran a hand down his face.

"Shit, sorry. This has been a helluva roller coaster day. And no, not in my family either," Brax answered, and he and I both waited for Mac to explain.

"First, twins come from the mother's side. What you are more likely looking at is mono amniotic twins. It happens when the egg splits. They are always identical, and they aren't as uncommon as you would think. The average is three to five out of a thousand births."

Mac continued to explain how identical twins were almost always the same sex. Not that there weren't document sets with one of each sex, they were rare. I listened as she said she was going to admit me overnight because of the concussion and she'd feel better if I was where they could monitor me. She printed a couple pictures from the ultrasound, then removed the wand and helped me get situated on the bed.

"I told you at your appointment today that we would get an ultrasound scheduled to determine a delivery date. That date is included on the picture. I will have Bailey schedule you another one, though. You'll be far enough along we should be able to tell the sex. Well, unless they move around and hide that information from us." Mac winked, and I laughed.

Mac sent the nurse to arrange a room for me, then wheeled the machine outside the curtain.

"Mac, will you go to the waiting area and let my brothers, and I'm sure by now their ol' ladies, know about Luna? And that she'll be in a room soon. I don't want to leave her," Brax asked.

"You bet. But I'll leave the little surprise for you guys to share. Congrats, both of you," Mac said and walked out.

Brax framed my face with his hands and kissed me. My life had changed so much in under two months because of this man. I wrapped my arms around his neck and enjoyed the feel of his mouth on mine. He broke the kiss and let go of my face, only to tuck his between my neck and shoulder. The whispered "Thank you" was said hoarsely.

191

"Ah, sweetie, I think I'm the one who should say that. But seriously, Brax, what the hell are we going to do with two?" My question had the right effect.

He straightened and smiled. "Hell, I guess a day at a time."

"At least I know why my jeans were tight this morning. My ass is going to be huge."

"Gives me more to hold on while I take you from behind." I smacked his stomach, and he placed his hand on the spot and rubbed as if I'd hurt him. When it was my hand that stung.

"If one time without a condom has me popping out duplicates, I'm going on the pill, AND you will wrap up after these babies are born." The man had the audacity to chuckle, and I glared at him.

"Baby, I was a SEAL. They trained me to do things right the first time."

"Oh my God, Lance said something like that to Bailey." I laughed.

"Hey, the military trained us well," he said and winked.

"Ready to move to your room?" a nurse asked as she walked in with an orderly behind her. I nodded, then she turned to Brax. "If you'll give us about twenty minutes to get her settled, you can join her in room 312."

"Sure. See you upstairs, baby. I'll go out to the waiting area and let the others know where they're moving you to," Brax said, then leaned over and kissed me.

The nurse and orderly unlocked the wheels on the bed and rolled the bed out of the cubicle behind Brax. I wondered as they pushed me down the hall to the elevators how long it would take Brax to spill the beans about the babies. I'd find out soon enough when the women could visit my room.

They settled me in my room, and the nurse had just filled my water pitcher when Brax walked through the door, followed by Max.

"You look no worse for wear," Max said, then leaned over the bed and kissed me on the cheek. "Congratulation, honey."

"Get your lips off my woman before you need a hospital bed, Flirt," Brax said, and the nurse smiled and winked at me on her way to the door.

"Figured I'd see her before the others get here and the women take over," Flirt said, and Brax sneered.

"Seeing is not your lips on her." Max chuckled at Brax when he shoved him out of the way to take his spot by the bed.

"Does anyone know if the person in the pickup was hurt?" I asked.

"Gunther Thurman. Hell no, he wasn't hurt. The bastard is too mean for that to happen," Carly said as she walked in with the other women behind her. Each carrying something. Carly set a vase with flowers on the table by the bed. Sami brought magazines, and Bailey carried snacks.

"Can we hug Luna and congratulate her on the twins before you go into details?" Sami said as she and Bailey came to the bed and hugged me.

Brax grinned when I looked at him. I smiled back. I'd called it. He wouldn't be able to keep it to himself.

"The brother folded as soon as he walked in the waiting area and I asked how you were holding up. He sang like a canary." Max laughed when Brax punched his arm.

"At least he didn't tell all of us to not say anything as if we didn't know like Lance did," Bailey said and rolled her eyes. "I thought my mom was going to disown me. Yelling she was the last to know."

When the women had first visited and helped me unpack, Bailey had confirmed Carly's suspicion and told Carly, Sami, and I that she was pregnant. We'd thought we knew something the guys didn't. We'd been wrong. It seemed even though Bailey and Lance talked about waiting to tell everyone, Bailey was the only one who had kept it to herself because Lance had already shared it with his dad and his brothers. Claire, Bailey's mom, had been upset about that but hadn't been able to stay that way when she thought about it not changing the fact she was going to be a grandma.

"Hey, if it helps, she ripped Dad up one side and down the other, because he knew and hadn't said shit," Flirt said and laughed. "I'm kind of sorry I missed it."

"Since they're only keeping you overnight, the guys said they'd check on you at home tomorrow," Carly said, then sat on the edge of the bed on one side and Bailey sat on the other side. Sami moved and sat in the only chair in the room.

"And Shakes, Sue, and a few of the other women are cooking, so you can rest. Said to tell you they will be by to see you," Bailey said. "Mom said she would drop off a cheesecake."

"I can feel my hips growing wider with just the thought of that cheesecake," I said and felt Brax's hand run over my hair.

"Baby, while the women are visiting, I'm going to go check on a few things. Be back in about an hour."

"Okay," I said, and he and Max left.

"God, he looks and sounds a lot better than when he walked into the ER."

"Carly," Sami scolded.

"Well, he does. His face was pale, and he had a stricken expression on his face. When he came back out after getting to see you, his color was back, and he wore a huge smile. It'd been like witnessing Jekyll and Hyde," Carly said, and did a mock shudder.

"Mac said you were at the sheriff's station. Did the other driver, whatever you said his name was, call in the accident?" I asked.

"Yes, I was picking up the paperwork needed to return to work when the call came in. The car behind you saw the whole thing happen. Gunther, the asshole, was going to flee the scene. His plan changed when Roscoe and Bull pulled up to the scene, though. They'd been heading to the club. Roscoe said you came to a couple of times in the truck while they were waiting for the ambulance to get there. He was the one who gave the EMTs your name and informed them you were pregnant," Carly said.

"I remember coming around the curve and he was in my lane. Knee-jerk reaction on yanking the steering wheel," I said and touched the bandage at my brow.

"Oh yeah. Found out why the dumbass was doing there. About four months ago, Gunther was busted for running a puppy mill. It was a huge operation. He had something like six or seven adult German Shepherds he bred. Authorities went in and took possession of the animals to include two litters, but he must have hidden a pregnant female. He was in your lane because he had tried to toss a garbage bag over the embankment there. Roscoe and Bull found the bag. It had six puppies in it," Carly said disgustedly.

"Aww, poor babies." I never understood how people could mistreat animals.

"I know. Thank God they found the little things. Roscoe said he checked them out, and they didn't seem harmed. They were taken to the local animal shelter to be examined. The sheriff went to Gunther's place and picked up the female dog. She was half starved. Some of the brothers were talking in the waiting area about adopting one. I don't expect the pups to be homeless long. The momma will take longer to find a home. Hell, if I wasn't going back to work soon, I'd adopt her," Carly said sadly.

"I love dogs, but one would have to spend a lot of time alone, and that isn't fair to it," Bailey said.

"Ally would love one if there are any left. I'm going to talk with Kane," Sami said, and rubbed her hand over her stomach. "I always wanted a dog growing up, but my mom got sick, then my dad was busy with Haven and trying to raise two kids, so Reed and I never had any pets."

"Same with me. It was just my mom and me. She worked to support us, so she always said she didn't need another mouth to feed. But I hate that the momma dog may not find a home. I had to have hit my head really hard for even saying this, but I'm going to tell Brax that I want the momma when she's cleared to be adopted," I said, and the others chuckled.

"Well hell, you better ask now while he is still reeling from your accident," Carly said.

"That's mean, Carly," Sami chastised.

"Uh, no it isn't. I'm just saying, don't give him time to think about them having two newborns or he may not say yes to taking on a dog, too."

"Carly's got a point as much as it pains me to agree," Bailey said, then laughed at the glare Carly turned on her.

"Well, considering he didn't want me to work, which looks like he might get his way now—at least *after* the babies come. I might get my way with the dog, though," I said and smiled. The women looked at me, then started laughing.

"There you go. And Sami says I'm manipulative," Carly said.

"I like to call it inventive." I grinned.

The women stayed until Brax got back. He brought me a change of clothes and personal items with him. Other than a mild headache, I felt fine and would have much rather been sent home, even if I understood why they wanted to keep me overnight. However, having Brax to myself and stretched out beside me in the small bed made the experience tolerable. Not that it was something I'd want to repeat.

Chapter Twenty

Ghost

My lungs burned as I ran on the path that snaked in different directions on the club's land. At one time, it had probably been a trail when the place was a lodge set up for people who liked the outdoors and everything to do with it. Leaves crunched under my feet as I pushed myself deeper into the surrounding forest, turning in the direction the path took me.

Besides my labored breathing and the thudding of my feet hitting the ground, the only other sounds were the occasional bird or small animal that was disturbed by my presence.

It'd been five days since Luna was run off the road. Five days since the doctor said Luna, and the babies were fine. Five days of the woman making it harder to resist her. Like it hadn't already felt a lifetime since I laid her down and sank into her. How the hell was I expected to put aside the thought of how close I came to losing it all again? Especially when every night I shut my eyes, I saw the caved-in side of my truck.

"Jesus, I should get a goddamn medal for not hunting down and killing that fucker," I yelled as I slowed down. When I finally stopped, I bent and placed my hands on my knees and worked to slow my breathing.

My phone vibrated, and I straightened and pulled my phone out of my pocket.

"Yo."

"Have we not discussed your phone etiquette?"

"Fuck you, Flirt. What's up?"

"I should ask you that. Saw your big ass running in the woods behind the pond. Had to look twice, thought it was bigfoot at first."

"You should take your comedy act on the f'n road."

"Just worried about you, man. Pops said he's seen you pass by a couple of times this week. You only run when something is bothering. So... what's up?"

"When did you start gossiping like an old woman, brother," I said and pulled the hem of my t-shirt up and wiped my face.

"Evading won't work. Neither will insults."

"Got shit on my mind. That's all. I'll work it out," I said. This was what happened when a friend knew you too well. They saw too much.

"Brax, brother, she's fine. The babies are fine. Don't let the past rear its ugly head, man. I'm not discounting what happened to Stormy and BJ. It was tragic. You can't control what life dumps on you. But you got a second chance. Live it. And you can't if all you do is worry about crap you can't control."

"Yeah, I tell myself that. Then I look at her, and I want to wrap her in bubble wrap. I was gutted over Stormy and BJ. Losing Luna would end me. There would be no coming back for me, Max. I just want to take care of her and keep her safe."

"Got that. But guess what? It's not today. Wasn't last week either. Luna doesn't strike me as the type to want to be coddled. And you have been a mother hen since you brought her home," Flirt said.

"Has she said something?" I asked, and when there wasn't an immediate response, I looked at my phone to check if the call dropped. "Flirt?"

"Dammit, I might have overheard the women talking about Luna complaining that she can't take much more of your hovering."

Well shit.

"It's hard, man. I don't want to hurt her," I said, my voice low because I didn't want to admit my fear.

"Stop borrowing trouble. Go home, pet the dog, and snuggle with your woman. She's here, enjoy it. Besides, when the kids get here, the spontaneous sex is gone. At least that's what I hear Speed and Dev bitch about. No more bending your woman over the kitchen table just because you can."

"Jesus, you're a dick. Just when I think you were concerned, you had to ruin it. You were doing good with the support until then, too. You're getting soft in your old age, brother." I smiled and started walking back.

"You know, go home, and spend your time boohooing over the shit you've lost. Then get a beer and fucking cry in it. You have a woman who loves you. Two kids on the way. But do you see it that way? No, you focus on what it would be like not to have them."

"You're such an asshole," I said to Flirt.

"A second ago, I was a dick."

I smiled and started picking up my pace.

"But ya love me, man. Admit it," I said as I grinned.

"Fuck you, Brax."

The line went dead when Flirt hung up. I chuckled, then went from a trot to a run. I needed to get to the house. I suddenly had a shit ton of energy and never felt lighter on my feet. It might take time for the vision in my head to fade, but I wouldn't let it rule my life.

Flirt was right, Luna was here. Breathing and safe, and evidently, feeling neglected, though I'd spent every minute taking care of her for the past week.

When I would've stopped in the yard and worked to cool down, I kept going. I caught the door before it hit the wall.

Luna swung around from the sink where she stood with the dog at her feet. We'd only had the animal for forty-eight hours, and she was already attached to Luna. It took some work to get the shelter to let us adopt her so soon after. But the argument that the dog could gain weight just as easily at our house where she would get one-on-one attention versus living in a shelter swayed them. They examined her, spayed, and vaccinated her, then turned her over.

Luna decided the poor dog need a new name, so Karma was now a part of our family. Since keeping her had been what bit Gunther in the ass, it fit.

I skirted the island and stalked toward my woman. Karma raised her head and eyed me.

"Brax, did something happen?" Luna asked and frowned.

"No, everything is exactly as it should be. But I was informed I might be neglecting my woman," I said as I reached her, then wanted to laugh at the change in her expression.

"You haven—"

"Gonna take my woman to bed. Got a problem with that?" I asked, bent, and swept her off her feet. She sighed and laid her head on my shoulder.

"I'm down with that." She sniffed, then raised her head. "But, Brax, sweetie, you need a shower."

"Damn, I pulled my head out of my ass, and now you want to complain? But I'll cut you a break since I need to clean up. You can help me."

"Oh, well, carry on," Luna said as I continued through the house with her in my arms and Karma following us.

I climbed the steps, and when I reached our room, I closed the door and plopped Luna on her feet. Karma laid on her new pillow, and I led Luna into the bathroom.

While the water heated, I stripped her down, then removed my own clothes. With us both naked, I wasted no time getting her into the shower.

Enough time with her had been squandered.

I lifted Luna, and she wrapped her legs around my waist, and I stepped into the spray. After the water soaked us, I turned and placed her back against the wall, leaving the water from the shower to run down my back.

Using one arm and the wall to support her, I ran my hand over her hair, then left it behind her head as I bent and took her mouth with mine. I nipped her bottom lip until she opened, then plunged my tongue in, tasting every crevice with new desperation. I'd never tire of being with her.

I released her mouth, only to travel my lips until I reached the spot below her ear. She tilted her head, giving me better access, and I gently bit, then sucked before moving to her shoulder to lick the pebbled water off her skin.

My lips moved across her collarbone to her other shoulder and up, working my way back to her lips. She rolled her hips until my cock was sliding between her center. She was warm, wet, and mine.

I rocked my hips back and forth, hitting her clit with every stroke. A shiver ran through her body, and she moaned around my tongue. My cock ached to be inside her.

Breaking the kiss, I leaned my forehead against hers. "Not sure I can go slow. Want and need you too bad."

"Take me, Brax. I will not break."

"Make it up to you in bed, baby," I said and pushed inside until she took all of me.

Holding her tight, my hips thrusting, I pounded into her until my balls drew up.

"Oh my God, I'm close," Luna panted.

"Me too, baby. Take us there."

And she did. Rocking her hips, grinding down until she started to climax, and her pussy tightened around me. My body shook as I released everything I had into her.

"If running causes this. By God you will run every damn day," Luna said as she leaned her head on my shoulder as we tried to calm our breaths.

"A week and no sex was the cause. But, baby, talk to me next time if you've got an issue with me," I said.

"I'm sorry, I just wanted you to treat me as before. And even though you were with me, I didn't know how to reach you."

"Not sure you could have. I needed to work it through my head."

"Well, I'll tell you this. If a week without getting laid gets this result. Then I can't wait to see what you're gonna be like with the six weeks of refraining after the babies are born."

"Got plenty of time to prepare for that. I'll stock up on Chapstick for ya. Don't want your lips to dry out or crack from all the use they're going to get from blowing me." I laughed, and Luna bit my shoulder. "Oww!"

"Put me down and let's wash, then we can refuel before round two." I slipped out of her and let her body slide down mine.

"Gonna marry me, baby. Make an honest man out of me?" I asked before I let go of her.

"Now? Or can it wait until we're done in the shower? The water is getting cold."

"Is that a yes, Luna?" I asked and smacked her ass. "Because if it is, I'm not waiting. Doing that shit soon."

"How you can be sweet one minute and so damn bossy the next amazes me."

"Still not a fuckin' yes."

"I've loved you my whole life, Brax. Yes."

"Love you, too, Luna. And I wouldn't have accepted a no, anyway."

Luna laughed. "Smug bastard."

We finished our shower, threw on clothes, and made our way to the kitchen.

As I stood beside her while we threw together sandwiches, I realized how unpredictable life was. There were always going to be times when I felt the weight of it on my shoulders. But in the end, with the right person standing with me, it would never be more weight than I could carry.

Epilogue

Jag

Ghost and I pulled the bikes to the curb in front of the building the club recently purchased. Through the window, I saw the contractor had the division wall between the two places completed. It wouldn't be long before they were done.

After I dismounted, I grabbed the papers I needed from my saddlebags and joined Ghost and Luna on the sidewalk.

"I'm going to go into Yoga Sensual first and get Mrs. Wayne's signature on the lease, then I'll meet you next door," I said and turned toward the door to the other business.

"We'll go in with you. Luna wants to check if they offer a prenatal yoga class," Ghost said, and he and Luna moved behind me.

I reached for the handle on the door, but before I grabbed it, the door swung open, and I stumbled back as a body plowed into me. Ghost's quick reaction when he grabbed my shoulders was the only thing that kept me on my feet.

"Oh my, I'm so sorry," was said as I gathered my balance. When I looked at the woman who spoke, she was bent over, picking up her bag and the contents that had fallen out when she'd dropped it. From the look of her, I was surprised I hadn't sent her flying back through the door.

"No problem. Let me help," I said and bent, only to have the woman rise and clock me on the chin with her head. The contact was hard enough my teeth rattled. I grabbed my chin with my hand and tested to see if my jaw was intact, then straightened back up. When I did, green eyes stared at me from a face surrounded by a mass of red hair. "For fuck's sake, is it your life's mission to kill me, River?"

"Excuse me, but I was exiting the establishment. Not my fault you don't watch where you are going. Maybe you should pay better attention." There was the snotty voice that had been haunting my dreams for more nights than I cared to count and the reason I felt my blood pressure go up.

"Yeah, ya think, huh?"

River glared at me with her chin out, and I leaned my face down to hers.

"Maybe if you pulled that stick out of your—"

"Sorry to interrupt," Luna said loudly, and I stopped before finishing my sentence. "Here are a few more of your things." Luna held her arm out and handed River a few more items that had come from her bag.

"Thank you," River said in a soft tone and smiled tentatively at Luna. Then her smile grew as she looked behind Luna. "Oh, hi. Brax, right?"

"That's right. Window still working, okay? No problems raising and lowering it?" Ghost asked.

"No problem at all."

I gritted my teeth and stared at River while she talked with my brother and his ol' lady. She didn't seem to have a problem with my brother, so wasn't I the lucky bastard she'd focused her frost on?

"You're taking classes here?" Luna asked.

"Yes, are you thinking about joining? Mrs. Wayne is great. I'm River, by the way."

"Luna, and yeah, I'm looking to take a prenatal class if she offers one. If not, I might take a regular class and just skip the exercises that aren't recommended for pregnant women."

"Oh, that's great. Not that I know anything about being pregnant, but I have read it can help with labor and delivery."

"I've read that, too. And hope it helps because not into proving how much pain I can take."

"Totally agree. Well, I guess I should be on my way," River said, and I watched as she placed the things Luna handed her into her bag. When she looked up at me, the smile she had for Luna and Ghost was gone and replaced with a sneer.

"If you want to finish telling me about the stick up my ass, could you hurry? I'd like to get home and shower."

"Don't let me keep you from your shower," I said and glared at her, then I moved to the side and let her pass. After she was a few steps away, I added. "Because God knows you could use the hot water to melt some of the ice off."

If I hadn't been watching her walk away, I wouldn't have noticed her falter before she continued down the sidewalk. And if I noticed how the tight pants she wore made her ass look good, wasn't anyone's business but mine.

"Damn, if the sexual tension were any thicker between you two, I'd need a knife," Luna said as she moved to step into the yoga place.

"What?" I turned around to face Luna.

"More like needing a hose to break up a fight," Ghost said and followed Luna through the door.

"Men. How do any of you ever get laid?"

"Because women can't go without a dick," Ghost said, and I chuckled when Luna looked over her shoulder and glared at him.

I walked through the door and stopped beside Ghost. I looked at him and cocked my brow to see if he had a clue what the hell his woman was talking about. When he shrugged, at least I didn't feel like the only clueless man around.

"When we get laid, it is by finding a woman who is warm-blooded. Not looking to get frostbite on important parts that I would like to keep using," I said as we waited for Mrs. Wayne to finish talking with another lady.

Ghost chuckled, and Luna shook her head at me.

"Good grief, you two are so under each other's skin that there is only one end to it. And when both of you realize the attraction is mutual, anyone close will end up with second-degree burns from being in the vicinity," Luna said, then turned and addressed Mrs. Wayne when she walked up.

I decided Luna was crazy if she thought the woman had an attraction to me.

As for me, I wasn't interested in spending the time to see if the ice princess could be thawed out. And dreams, they would go away. Eventually.

Right?

Christ, a woman I barely knew punched buttons I didn't even know I had. And it pissed me off.

To even the playing field, maybe I needed to find her buttons and give them a push.

Acknowledgements

To everyone who has lost someone special in their life and felt as if life would never be the same. Second chances exist—you only need to be open to them.

Carson

About the Author

Carson Mackenzie enjoys writing romance with a real feel inside the stories. She writes with the belief not every man is a jerk and not every woman needs saving.

Carson lives in the South with one of her sons, a Great Dane and two adopted shelter dogs that keep the household in line. Books have always been a part of her life. There is nothing better to her than curling up and relaxing with a good story and losing herself in someone else's world for a few hours.

Writing stories and growing as an author with each book is her goal. She wants to reach the level where a reader knows when they see her name, they can trust in the fact there will be a good story as they flip through the pages.

Carson's been her writing journey for a few years. As she's finally starting to settle in, her only regret is she hadn't started sooner.

To stay up to date with Carson – visit her website- https://carsonmackenzieauthor.com/ or sign up for her newsletter- https://landing.mailerlite.com/webforms/landing/l2k1l8.

Books by Carson Mackenzie

Black Hawk MC

Speed
Crusher
Devil
Ghost
Jag
Coast
Flirt

Haven MC

Moose's Regret
Hawk's Bounty
Keg's Revelation

Desert Phoenix MC

Desert Phoenix Rising

Standalones

Her Way or No Way
two paths One destiny

Boxed Sets

Black Hawk MC Books 1-3
Black Hawk MC Books 4-7
Haven MC Books 1-3